The Beastly Duke's Convenient Bride

(Regency Expedient Marriages Book 1)

HISTORICAL REGENCY ROMANCE NOVEL

Dorothy Sheldon

Copyright © 2021 by Dorothy Sheldon
All Rights Reserved.
This book may not be reproduced or transmitted in any form without the written permission of the publisher. In no way is it legal to reproduce, duplicate, or transmit any part of this document in either electronic means or in printed format. Recording of this publication is strictly prohibited and any storage of this document is not allowed unless with written permission from the publisher.

Table Of Contents

The Beastly Duke's Convenient Bride 1
Prologue 4
Chapter One 9
Chapter Two 13
Chapter Three 20
Chapter Four 28
Chapter Five 35
Chapter Six 43
Chapter Seven 51
Chapter Eight 58
Chapter Nine 65
Chapter Ten 72
Chapter Eleven 79
Chapter Twelve 86
Chapter Thirteen 94
Chapter Fourteen 98
Chapter Fifteen 105
Chapter Sixteen 113
Chapter Seventeen 121
Chapter Eighteen 127
Chapter Nineteen 133
Chapter Twenty 139
Chapter Twenty-One 144
Chapter Twenty-Two 148
Chapter Twenty-Three 152
Chapter Twenty-Four 156
Chapter Twenty-Five 161
Chapter Twenty-Six 166
Chapter Twenty-Seven 171
Chapter Twenty-Eight 176
Chapter Twenty-Nine 180
Chapter Thirty 184

Epilogue 188
Extended Epilogue 192

Prologue

London, Ten Years Ago

The snow was pelting down outside. What had started as a wet flurry of snow only that morning had turned into something decidedly harsher and colder.

It was windy, too, an icy gale that howled around Blackburn Manor, getting it cold fingers through any gaps it could find. Sitting in the bare hallway outside his father's rooms, Adam shivered.

He hadn't moved for hours, expecting any minute to hear the news he'd been dreading.

Or looking forward to, although Adam wouldn't let himself think that way.

He'd be proud of me if I did, though, he thought, smiling bitterly.

Shifting his feet, which seemed to be almost literally frozen to the stone floor, Adam wondered how much longer he should wait. The house was virtually in mourning already.

The door, heavy oak and scarred with age and use, creaked open. Adam flinched, sitting bolt upright, as though he expected his father to appear and bellow at him for hunching over.

Gentlemen don't slouch, boy!

It was only the physician, though. Doctor Mulberry was a faded, colourless sort of man, with whitish-grey hair and a thin, pale face. He had a habit of wringing his hands together and tended to do it all the more when faced with an imposing person, or a troublesome patient.

The poor man had almost wrung his hands raw over the past week.

"How is he?" Adam asked. His voice sounded obscenely loud in the quiet hallway. Not a sound came from inside the bedroom. For a wild moment Adam thought that perhaps Lord Hector Blackburn, the Duke of Brixham, had left the world already, without sparing a moment to say goodbye to his only child, his heir.

"Not good." Doctor Mulberry said, his whispery voice sounding tired. "It won't be long now, I'm afraid. There's nothing further I can do for him. He wants to see you."

Adam swallowed. "I see. Should I go in now? What should I do?"

Doctor Mulberry blinked, shrugging his thin shoulders. "Sit by his bedside, I suppose. I must say, young people don't usually need to ask what to do when confronted by their dying parents."

That was a rebuke, and Adam felt himself wanting to shrink back, to hunch his shoulders and apologise. He could only imagine how furious the Duke would be at his son behaving that way.

Remember your training, Adam told himself. He stood a little taller, squaring his shoulder and fixing Doctor Mulberry with a steely, ice-blue gaze. He had his father's eyes, and knew from experience how penetrating that glare could be.

"I beg your pardon?" Adam said, and Doctor Mulberry visibly shrank back.

"I... I didn't mean to imply..."

"But you did, didn't you? Please do remember your place, Doctor. I don't take kindly to implications."

That was the sort of thing that the Duke would say. He'd be proud, Adam thought.

Doctor Mulberry swallowed, bobbing his head in what was either a vigorous nod or a shallow bow, and scurried away. Adam felt the familiar twinge of regret, speaking to someone else like that, but it was disappearing more and more quickly these days.

Then there was nothing left but to push open the bedroom door and go inside.

The Duke's room was opulent, but not overwhelmingly so. With the thick curtains across the windows, very little light got into the room. Even so, Adam knew that the blocky shapes of furniture represented valuable antiques, even priceless ones.

A single candle burned beside the bed; a huge four-poster draped in red velvet to match the curtains.

It was easy to miss the man huddled inside. The illness had come suddenly, stripping away the layers of fat and muscle from the Duke. He was still taller than Adam, even at the end, but it was a shrunken husk of a man who greeted him now. A thin hand, covered in dry, papery skin, extended itself from the bedsheets. It took Adam a moment to realize that his father was holding out his hand, wanting his son to take it.

This was another first.

Adam took the grasping hand automatically, and the movement felt strange.

"My boy," the Duke rasped. "It's good to see you."

Adam's throat clenched. It's good to see you. He didn't think he'd ever heard his father say that to him. The man before him didn't look like his father, not without the familiarly grim, set expression on his face. The sick man was almost smiling, face lit up with relief at the sight of his son. His voice had changed, too – it was a rasping, feeble warble now, not the deep, demanding tone that Adam was used to.

He cleared his throat, hoping that his father wouldn't see the changing expression on his face.

"Yes, Father, I'm here. How are you feeling?"

The Duke gave a snort. "Let's not waste time talking about that. I'm dying, and we all know it."

Now here was the Duke of Brixham that Adam knew. Here was his father, sharp and dismissive.

"We don't know that." Adam said, despite himself.

He received a steely glare for his troubles.

"We do know that. Don't be stupid, boy. I'm not the sort of deny the plain facts of a thing, no matter how vexing they might be. I hadn't intended to die for a good long while yet. God, you are barely eighteen, and far from ready. Oh well, there's not a great deal we can do about that. There's so much more you had to learn, and it's not my concern anymore how you come to learn the rest. Time, in its irritating way, has evaded me. You'll be the Duke of Brixham when I'm gone, today or tomorrow, and heaven only knows how you'll manage."

"I'll manage." Adam said, stung. "You've taught me how to manage."

"Yes, I suppose you will." the Duke said, with a raspy chuckle. "You're a better man than I was at your age."

Adam blinked. Was that... was it a compliment? After that sharp, unforgiving speech about how Adam wouldn't be able to 'manage'? Had his father just praised him?

Adam's throat clenched, and tears pricked threateningly at his eyes. He ground his teeth, forcing himself to stay composed. He wouldn't let his father down now. He'd show him that he was the staid, serious man he was meant to be.

I can do it.

The Duke coughed, a horrible rattling noise that almost sounded like bubbling in his lungs.

"I... I haven't got long, boy. You remember what I told you, you hear me? You remember. You will, won't you?"

"I will, Father, I will." Adam promised, glad that it was too dark for his father to see the moisture glittering in his eyes. "I'll be a good Duke. I promise. I'll do whatever I have to. Whatever it takes. I'll be whatever you wanted me to be."

The light was fading out of the Duke's eyes.

"Good," he murmured, the words barely more than a breath. "Good."

With that, the old Duke of Brixham faded away, his final exhale a long, drawn-out thing. The room seemed quieter without his rattling breaths.

Adam allowed himself no more than ten minutes to grieve. Even that felt excessive. A flurry of emotion that his father would not have approved of. The Duke hadn't mourned his wife for that long, although of course Adam hadn't been privy to most – or indeed, any – of his father's feelings on the subject.

The ten minutes elapsed, and Adam of conscious of a guilty feeling of relief. No point wasting time now, was there? Suddenly decided, he placed his father's hand back on the sheets and stood up. There was a lot of work to do, starting – but certainly not limited to – the funeral. It would need to be an elaborate affair, and Adam would need to figure out exactly how long he would need to wear black. Mourning was annoying – his father had said so, more than once – but it was mandatory. When it came to mourning one's father, one ought to err on the side of caution. Society was eagle-eyed when it came to spotting faults, and it was notoriously unforgiving.

He wouldn't go into half-mourning until it was absolutely safe for him to do so. It was a formality, and one that would hopefully pass quickly. Adam did not feel like mourning his father for too long. The old Duke would not have expected him to.

The new Duke of Brixham strode out into the hallway, never once looking back.

Chapter One

Present Day, London, Springtime

It was a good party. Everyone said so, even the snobby gossips and Society Beauties that made a point of being bored and disinterested with everything. Of course, they wouldn't openly admit that they were enjoying themselves.

Marina could always tell, of course. She had a knack for sniffing out lies and other deceits – her Papa said so. He'd taught her how to read people, how to eye them subtly over a hand of cards and work out whether they planned to fold or up their bet. He'd taught her how to make them think that she was going to do one thing, and then react blandly to their shock when she did the opposite.

"Play the player, girl, not the cards," he'd said once, grinning. "Every hand is a winning one, and every hand is a losing one. It all depends on who holds them, and how well they read the table. It's a skill, make no mistake, but one that involves a heavy dose of luck."

It wasn't appropriate for ladies to learn those sorts of card games, but Marina didn't mind. In her opinion, what she and her family did in their own drawing rooms were nobody's business but their own. It was better than painting watercolours or practising the same fashionable minuets over and over again.

Or worse, poring over an "improving" book for hours on end, pretending to be interested. Novels were fashionable but frowned upon at the same time, and no self-respecting young lady who aspired to Cleverness would admit reading them.

No, Marina would much rather play cards. She was good at cards, and it was like a little secret they all kept together. Even her Mama played a few hands now and then, although most of the time she just sat in her chair, sighing dramatically and shaking her head, trying not to laugh at her ridiculous family.

They didn't gamble for real money, after all – just sweets or beads or something. They were always fun, too. Marina enjoyed those evenings the most, full of laughter and silly inside jokes and just enough pieces of really good advice.

"See, Rina, when someone glances up like this, it means that they're lying."

"Really? You can tell that just by where they put their eyes?"

"Oh yes, little one. That's only the start of what you can learn about a person."

Marina hid a smile in her champagne glass. She had no idea where her parents were now. The party was hosted by one of her mother's friends – her mother, Letitia Cornish, Countess of Chelwood, seemed to know everyone – and that was why they were invited. Lately, the Cornish star seemed to be on the decline. They'd once been one of the foremost families, but now the invitations were starting to dwindle away. Marina had no idea what was wrong. She was barely twenty, and this was only her second Season, so she was hardly a ridiculous spinster just yet. What was going on behind the scenes?

She was jerked out of her thoughts as the dance finished. The musicians ended the song with a flourish, and the dancers stopped whirling around, and broke out in applause. Marina smiled thinly, trying to tamp down the feelings of jealousy.

She wouldn't have minded dancing, but so far there was only one name on her dance card, and that was her father's. Samuel Cornish would never let his daughters go through a whole ball without dancing with anyone.

Not that it mattered for Josephine yet – she wasn't Out, and wouldn't come Out until Marina was respectably married.

That didn't seem likely to be happening anytime soon. This was Marina's second Season, and while she didn't believe she was shockingly plain or entirely unsociable, nobody had yet arrived to make her heart skip a beat.

That was what Marina wanted. She wanted to marry a man she loved, and to have a happy, chaotic life like her parents. Scanning the ranks of assembled gentlemen in the ballroom, her heart sank. No hopes of finding her Prince Charming here. Some ladies had whispered eagerly about their hopes that the handsome, eligible Duke of Brixham would arrive, but that had come to nothing.

Marina wasn't acquainted with the Duke and didn't particularly wish to be. She knew him by reputation, and it seemed like he was a cold, ruthless gentleman, and not somebody she'd care to meet.

None of it mattered, of course, since the elusive Duke had not arrived.

"Ah, Marina! There you are! There she is, you see. I told you she'd be here."

Marina flinched, turning at the sound of Lord Chelwood, her father, ambling his way through the crowd towards her.

Samuel was a short gentleman, round-faced and decidedly portly in his later years. He had the same chestnut-brown hair and bright green eyes that he'd bequeathed to Marina, although the skin of his face was reddened with too much drinking and good living. He beamed at Marina, although there was a tightness in the corners of his eyes, as if the smile was entirely forced.

Her smile faded. Hadn't he taught her to spot these tiny mannerisms in people, to work out their intentions?

She didn't have time to think more on it, because Samuel was then in front of her, followed by a tall, starving-thin gentleman of about forty.

"Marina, my dear, you remember Lord Charles Ellersby, don't you?" Samuel said, his voice entirely too bright.

Marina smiled politely, dropping a curtsey.

She did, indeed, remember Lord Ellersby. Aside from being tall and thin, Lord Ellersby had a strangely pale and gaunt face, skin stretched over his face tight enough to make him look like a skeleton. He had colourless grey hair that might once have been blond, thinning and plastered unflatteringly against his scalp. His nose was too large for his face, and his nostrils flared wide when he breathed in, as if he were trying to take in the scent of the person he was speaking to.

At the moment, he seemed to be trying to take in Marina's scent. He extended a hand, fingers too long and white, and she reluctantly took it. His skin was clammy, and he bent over her hand with a flourish. She felt dry, thin lips brush her knuckles, and tried not to shiver.

Everything about Lord Ellersby sent her skin a-prickle. He was an occasional visitor at their house, and Letitia didn't seem to like him any better than Marina. Why Samuel insisted on keeping his company, Marina did not know. Although at the moment, Samuel was flashing uncertain looks at Lord Ellersby, fidgeting as if he wanted to shuffle away.

That wasn't at all how friends acted with each other.

"You are not dancing, Lady Cornish." Lord Ellersby said smoothly. "It is a great pity to see a pretty young thing like you standing on the sidelines."

Marina didn't much like being called a pretty young thing, but she smiled politely again.

"I'm sure there'll be opportunities to dance later in the evening." She said, which seemed like a suitably vague thing to say. Marina was no fool, and she could already tell what Lord Ellersby intended to ask. She could see it in the twitch of his long fingers, and the predatory glint in his eyes.

She wished that she could say no. Judging by the anxious way Samuel kept looking at her, he was afraid that she might say no.

Why?

"Perhaps there may be an opportunity to dance now. Would you care to join me for the next set, Lady Cornish?"

There it was. The invitation she had been dreading.

Marina smothered a sigh. She couldn't very well refuse his offer to dance. Gentlemen did the asking, and of course wouldn't ask any lady they didn't like to dance with them, but there was no provision for a lady to refuse a dance.

Of course, she could plead a twisted ankle or tiredness, but then there must be no dancing for the rest of the evening. Even then, it was shockingly impolite.

"Of course." Marina said, as if there was anything else she could have said in reply. "I should like that."

Lord Ellersby's smile widened.

Chapter Two

Matthew dropped the heavy tome onto the desk in front of Adam, raising a huge cloud of dust.

"The debtors' book, your Grace." Matthew intoned. "Or rather, the latest copy of it. I believe this book covers this year, from January to now. If you wish to see earlier copies, then I can..."

"No, no, thank you, Matthew." Adam coughed, ineffectually waving away the dust. "This is the one I wanted."

Matthew slunk back against the wall, watching in that intent, impassive way of his. The man scarcely seemed to blink.

It didn't bother Adam. He'd long since ceased to be unsettled by his estate steward. Matthew was around fifty and was a stick-thin man with a completely bald head and unsettlingly deep-set eyes. He'd been the estate steward here for as long as Adam could remember, and it seemed entirely natural for Adam to keep him on once the old Duke was dead.

They didn't particularly like each other. Matthew unsettled Adam, and he was fairly sure that Matthew thought him a spoilt upstart, still a boy even at the age of twenty-eight. Still, Matthew knew that he wouldn't be unceremoniously removed from his post in favour of someone younger, and Adam could recognize a clever, efficient person when he saw one, and Matthew was certainly an exceptional estate steward.

Adam opened the book, turning to the page he wanted. He mumbled to himself under his breath, eye skipping down the long columns of debtors on one side, the sums owing on the other. Some people had all but paid off their debts, and others still had thousands more to pay. Plus interest, of course. Some names appeared over and over again, others just once. Adam was familiar with all of them.

He paused at one particularly entry, tapping the name.

"Have we heard from the Earl of Chelwood, Matthew?" Adam asked. "I sent him a message a full week ago, asking to meet up."

"No, your Grace."

"Hm. Has he paid any of what he owes?"

"No, your Grace."

Adam frowned, leaning back in his seat. Without any payments, the figure on the right column would only grow, until it became such a sickeningly large number that only total bankruptcy would repay the debt.

Or worse.

"I hope he doesn't think I'm a soft touch." Adam muttered. "I'll send him to Marshalsea, and good riddance to him. I've sent members of the ton there before, and never thought twice about it."

The Earl of Chelwood was one of the nicer clients Adam had done business with. He was a jovial, friendly man, who didn't seem to understand that walking into a money-lender's house was not unlike walking into a lion's den. Adam had liked him, as well as he could like the greedy fools who borrowed his money at such high rates.

Lord Chelwood's business idea had been sound – breeding stallions had the potential to be a lucrative venture, and Lord Chelwood had a notable knack for spying out good horseflesh. If Adam did not see a return on his investment soon, he would do whatever it took to recover his money.

I'm no fainting dandy, Adam thought grimly. I'll take my pound of flesh.

"Matthew, what is the gossip like about the earl's financial situation at the moment? Is it possible he's simply missed a payment?"

Matthew shot Adam a pitying look.

"Not good, your Grace. Word has it that he is struggling financially. People are beginning to notice, and he is making increasingly more desperate efforts to collect money together."

Adam sighed, closing his eyes. He'd heard this story before. A gentleman, having fallen upon difficult times, borrows too much money at too high an interest rate. His business plan, for whatever reason, fails. He panics and tries to resort to gambling and cards to scrape the money together to repay the moneylender.

It never worked.

Adam raked a hand through his dark hair, suddenly feeling as if every limb was weighed down with something heavy. He felt bone tired. The clock on the wall read a quarter to twelve at night. To think that he'd hoped to have an early finish today.

"Well, we'll need to set up a meeting with the earl." Adam said. "One way or another. I'm running out of patience with him. For now, you'd better get yourself to bed. It's late."

Matthew gave a shallow bow, and slipped noiselessly out of the door, closing it softly behind him. Maybe he was tired – it was hard to spot emotions on that cadaverous face.

Adam stayed where he was, staring at the entry in the debtor's book, tapping the end of his pencil on the desk. He hoped that the earl wouldn't find himself in the book of bad debts.

He didn't particularly like sending his debtors to Marshalsea. That prison was infamous, and unnecessarily cruel. But what was he meant to do? Adam had little to no patience with those who borrowed what they could not repay. The old Duke had felt exactly the same, and carefully instilled those values in his son.

"For every action, there is consequence." Adam muttered. "Everyone that borrows must repay, one way or another."

Still, he'd rather be repaid with the money he was owed, rather than throwing the debtor in question into prison. Then the money would never be repaid.

That is not the point, stated a voice in the back of Adam's head, sounding strangely like his father's voice, back when he was in good, firm health. The point is to make an example. It is the principle of the thing.

And Adam had already sent men to prison or the depths of bankruptcy on the basis of principle.

The clock in the corner struck midnight, making Adam jump. He stared at it, a little bewildered.

Where had the day gone?

On cue, the door flew open with a crash. Only one person would enter his study without knocking, and in such a dramatic fashion.

"Hello, Mother." Adam said. "And how are you this evening?"

Evelyn Blackburn, the Dowager Duchess, was an exceptionally beautiful woman, even at the age of forty-six. Sometimes, she attracted more attention than the younger ladies. She had thick black hair, only just beginning to streak with silver, brown eyes, and olive skin that tanned deeply in summer. Tanned skin was unfashionable, of course, but somehow Evelyn had always managed to look beautiful anyway. Adam often wondered what had possessed her to marry his father.

Money, probably. And family pressure.

They hadn't been a happy couple, he knew that. Evelyn had barely been eighteen when she was married, and Adam was born only a few weeks before her nineteenth birthday. The old Duke was considerably older, and quickly lost interest in his wife once his son appeared. From a young age, Adam had noticed the disparity between his parents, the abject disinterest they showed in each other. Now, of course, he knew that many marriages were like that. It was silly to believe that a marriage among the ton would end otherwise.

"I am not happy, Adam. Not happy at all." Evelyn stated. "Can you guess why?"

"I'm sure that you are about to tell me."

Evelyn pressed her lips together, obviously displeased. Adam laced his fingers together on top of the debtor's book and tried to look innocent.

Of course, he knew why she was upset. There'd been some party or soiree that night that he apparently should not have missed. Adam disagreed. He could miss any or all of those dreadful events and suffer no consequences. Not to mention that it was an absolute waste of an evening. He'd much rather sit with a book and a glass of brandy by his fireplace, than cram into an overcrowded ballroom and make inane small talk all evening.

"You promised you would come." Evelyn said. Now she didn't sound angry, just disappointed, and the first waves of guilt rolled over him.

"I'm sorry, Mother. I didn't say that I would come, by the way. I said I might come."

"Oh, tosh! You led me to believe that you would be there."

Adam sighed, twirling his pencil in his fingers.

"Somehow, I don't think I would be well-received at an event like that. Half of the people there owe me money."

"Oh, Adam!"

"I am sorry to disappoint you, Mother. There was just so much work to be done."

"There is always 'so much work to be done'. It never ends." Evelyn responded tartly. She pulled out a chair opposite Adam's desk and threw herself down. She was wearing a dark blue satin dress, well-fitted and pretty, that glistened in the candlelight. She must have looked splendid at the party.

She shouldn't have come back for me, Adam thought with a pang. She could have been out there, enjoying herself. Goodness know that she enjoys socialising.

"I'm worried about you, Adam." Evelyn stated.

He raised his eyebrows. "About me? Why?"

"Why do you think? You spend all day and most of the night poring over those wretched books, shut up in here with that awful steward of your father's. You're pale and tired, and you seem more and more discontented with each passing day."

Adam considered arguing the point about spending all day and most of the night working, but considering the fact it was now just past midnight, he felt that he could not win that argument.

"And you think that going to these inane parties will make me more contented, will it?"

She shrugged. "At any rate, it'll get you away from those books."

"I'm quite happy here, Mother. I have work to do."

"You always have work to do. Besides," she hesitated, leaning forward. "You won't find a wife in those debtor's columns, will you?"

He let out a bark of laughter. "What on earth makes you think I'm shopping for a wife?"

Evelyn flashed a tight-lipped smile. "Because you are dangerously close to thirty, and you still have no heir. Do you want the estate and title to go to your cousin?"

Adam winced. "I certainly do not."

"You're running out of time to secure a legacy, Adam. You're not a fool, I know that you must have considered that."

Adam stared at the pencil, still twisting and spinning in his fingers.

"Look, Mother, you've seen the young ladies in Society today. They're just... well, there's nothing there. They're pretty, and people say that they're accomplished, but that's all. I've never felt drawn to any of them. I felt like a fool, doggedly attending all those ridiculous balls and soirees, waiting for some sort of connection with someone or other. It's never arrived, and I now believe that it never will."

Evelyn bit her lip. "I'm sorry, darling. I wanted to marry for love too, but... well, it didn't happen. You know that. sometimes these things just don't work out. Perhaps you just need to abandon this notion of a connection and just pick someone suitable. Perhaps love will come later."

Adam leaned forward, resting his elbows on his desk.

"Mother, you know that people hate me, don't you? Everyone knows someone who borrowed money from me and then was shocked when I had the audacity to force them to pay it back. They don't like me. They're afraid of me. And to be frank, I like that. I don't care to have these people's respect. I have your respect, and your affection, and that is all I care about."

Evelyn reached across the desk, taking his hand in hers.

"You might one day meet a woman who inspires your respect. And your affection, perhaps."

"Perhaps." He echoed, but it was hollow. "I don't want to marry for the sake of it."

Evelyn's face hardened. "You are not marrying for the sake of it. Really, Adam, you can be selfish at times. Is there to be no legacy? Are you really so short-sighted? Dukes marry, and they have children. That is the way it's always been, because we have a tradition to carry on. We have estates and titles that must be passed onto the next generation. Time is running out for you, Adam. Already you're something of a black sheep in Society. I want to see you happy, and I believe that doing your duty here will give you a measure of contentment."

Adam sat back, withdrawing his hand.

"I'm not a child, Mother. I will do what I see fit, and I don't believe that forcing myself into a pointless marriage is the best thing for me. Or for anyone, for that matter. It's hardly fair, in any case. Please, I'd be obliged if you'd keep your advice to yourself in this matter."

He's spoken too harshly. Adam could have bitten of his tongue the moment the words left his lips, but of course it was far too late. Evelyn turned scarlet, flinching back as if he'd struck her.

"Of course." she said, her voice cold and tight. "How foolish of me to think that I, your mother, could possibly have anything worthwhile to suggest. Sometimes, Adam, you are so much like your father it is quite shocking."

Adam knew his mother well enough to know what an insult that was. He was still reeling when she got to her feet, pushing back the chair with a screech, and hurried to the door.

"Mother, wait!" he called. "Please, I'm sorry. I shouldn't have..."

He was cut off by the door slamming. Adam let out a sigh, sinking down in his seat. The clock merrily chimed half-past twelve.

He'd never sleep now.

Chapter Three

Two Days Later, Chelwood Manor

"I can't believe you get to go to the party, and I have to go to bed." Josephine moaned.

Marina raised an eyebrow, looking at her sister through the mirror.

"Actually, you should already be in bed now."

Josephine shrugged, picking up a hairpin and inspecting it.

"Well, you aren't going to tell, are you? Will I get to come as soon as you're married?"

"You're coming out next year, whether I'm married or not." Marina replied, ignoring the pang of nostalgia. Where had her grubby tomboy of a little sister gone? Josephine was now seventeen and was blossoming into a pretty young lady.

She had their mother's hair, thick, glossy, and jet-black. Paired with their father's remarkable hazel eyes, she would cut quite a handsome figure in Society.

Marina turned her attention back to her own reflection. It was clear that Letitia had spared no expense with their party tonight. The food was plentiful, the champagne was flowing, and a set of extremely expensive musicians would be playing. She felt a flutter of excitement at the thought of the evening. There was always the chance that some mysterious stranger would arrive – it would have to be a stranger, since Marina already knew all of the eligible men and was not impressed with any of them – and sweep her off her feet.

It would be pleasant to be taken away from all this, from whatever kept Samuel awake and pacing the halls at night, and whatever secret lurked behind Letitia's eyes. Something was going on, and whatever it was, her parents were not going to share it with her.

They were more keen than ever for her to make a good match, and Marina wanted more than anything else to make her parents happy, and pave the way for Josephine to be happy, too.

Was it so wrong to want some happiness for herself, though?

"You look very pretty." Josephine said approvingly. "Put that tortoise-shell comb in your hair."

Marina was wearing a light, sea-foam green dress that frothed and swayed around her like real sea waves. It was a simple design, but she knew that it flattered her. In this light, her eyes would look properly green, not just hazel. Laughing, she picked up the comb Josephine had picked out, and delicately placed it by her temple.

"How's that?" she asked, spinning around in a circle.

Josephine grinned. "Perfect."

***

The ballroom and the dining room looked like fairyland. Candles glittered like stars, paper flowers hung from the ceiling (well away from the candles, of course), and there were garlands of real flowers everywhere, filling the room with a sweet fragrance.

The heat was oppressive, and there was a terrible crush of people, but that was generally seen as the sign of a ball's success. Marina weaved her way through the crowd, smiling and greeting various acquaintances. Everyone in Society had endless acquaintances, but Marina was not one of those who were lucky enough to have friends, too.

Oh, well. Nothing to be done about that. Society was a trite place, and anyone who said otherwise was either a liar or a fool.

Maybe both.

"Ah, there you are, Lady Cornish!"

Marina's heart sank into her stomach. She debated pretending not to have heard and pushing her way on through the crowd but knew deep down that it was already too late. She could practically feel cool breath fanning across the back of her neck.

She turned, slowly, pasting a polite but uninviting smile on her face.

"Lord Ellersby. Good evening."

He was smiling down at her with that same predatory grin. What on earth did he want from her? Surely not marriage. He was far too old.

Even as she thought that, Marina's memory conjured up half a dozen teenage acquaintances of hers who had married men or forty and fifty, with their parents' enthusiastic consent. Ugh.

"I was looking for you." Lord Ellersby continued. "We never had time to converse after our dance the other night, did we?"

Marina, who had done her level best to escape his clammy clutches even before the last notes of the dance were played, shook her head in wide-eyed innocence. "No, Lord Ellersby, we didn't."

"Well, we shall remedy that tonight. Let me see, do you have many dancing engagements tonight?"

Before Marina could say anything, he had reached out long, grasping fingers and neatly snatched the dance card off her wrist.

She knew fine well that he would be greeted with empty rows, with only Samuel's name down for a dance or two. Marina prayed that she would not blush.

Lord Ellersby's mouth twitched. "Well, this is a surprise. You are quite the hidden gem, Lady Cornish. Shall we say – the second and third set together? I daresay your Papa will want to open the ball with you. After that, you are all mine."

He handed the card back, making sure that his fingers brushed Marina's when she took it.

She saw all the smug satisfaction and anticipation of a man who was convinced that he'd already won. Marina had seen on her partner's face when she was losing a game of chess, and they both knew she was losing. She'd seen it on a friend who held a winning hand of cards.

This, however, was a game that Marina did not know how to play. That didn't mean that you couldn't lose, though.

"Of course." Marina managed, as if there was anything else to say.

"Fabulous! Let's take a turn around the room while we wait."

No escape, then.

Lord Ellersby drew Marina's limp arm through his, half-dragging, half escorting her towards a quiet corner near the mantelpiece.

Does he not see how much I dislike him, or does he not care? Marina wondered. Probably both.

"You are look lovely tonight, Lady Cornish." Lord Ellersby murmured, his lips far too close to Marina's ear. She repressed a shudder.

His breath was stale and laced heavily with alcohol. Now Marina better understood the spark in Lord Ellersby's eyes. She couldn't tell if he was in his cups or not – his hand was steady and he didn't slur his words – but he'd clearly drunk quite a lot before coming here tonight.

Sometimes, Samuel overindulged in alcohol. Gentlemen weren't supposed to let ladies see them in their cups, but really, Samuel was quite funny. Marina had heard it once said that alcohol brought out the person inside. Samuel's person inside was a giggly man who made deeply inappropriate jokes and recited terrible poems of his own concoction about his wife's beauty.

Somehow, Marina doubted that Lord Ellersby would be so amusing.

"I don't believe we've ever had a proper conversation." She found herself saying. "Why are you so keen for my company?"

That, of course, was deeply impolite, but Lord Ellersby's grin only widened.

"I think you are under the impression that your silence is off-putting. On the contrary, I find it most becoming. Beguiling, even."

Marina shuddered.

It was going to be a long evening.

***

It was going to be a long evening.

Adam watched his mother fiddle with her earrings, inspecting her reflection in the parlour mirror.

"I'm really not in the mood to entertain guests, Mother." Adam said mildly.

"Oh, come on, Adam. It's just Lord and Lady Rockwell. You remember, James and Susannah Sixsmith?"

"I don't remember them at all."

Evelyn sighed. "Well, you should. They're dear friends of mine, and I haven't seen them in far too long. I promised them that you would be here."

Adam wanted to scream.

Why? He wanted to ask. Why did you tell them I would be here? My company is hardly going to add anything to dinner.

Still, if he wanted to make up for his harsh words to his mother, Adam knew what he needed to do. He needed to greet her friends and be the perfect house host

"You might remember their daughter more clearly." Evelyn said, determinedly avoiding his gaze. "Olivia? She's around twenty-one, I believe."

Adam narrowed his eyes. "So that is what this is all about? You're trying to set me up with Olivia Sixsmith?"

Evelyn turned back from the mirror with an annoyed tut.

"I am doing nothing of the sort. Really, Adam, you ought not to be so suspicious. Oh, I think they're here!"

***

It took Adam about ten minutes to realize that Lord Rockwell was terrified of him.

The older man – short, portly, and with heavily waxed mustachios – kept glancing nervously in Adam's direction, and flinched whenever he spoke. Lady Rockwell was a chatterbox of a woman, single-handedly carrying the conversation. Olivia was extremely pretty, with the sort of fair, blonde curls that were so fashionable at the moment, a well-featured oval face, and a pale pink gown. Lady Rockwell took pains to describe her daughter as "musical" which Adam took to mean that the pianoforte would be opened at some point, for Olivia to display her talents.

He stared at Lord Rockwell for a long moment, eyes narrowed. He could almost see beads of sweat starting out on the man's forehead.

"Everything alright, your Grace?" Lord Rockwell managed, sounding constipated.

"Yes, yes. I'm just trying to think of whether I've seen you somewhere before. You look awfully familiar..." Adam mused.

Under the table, Evelyn kicked his shin. Adam decided that he had had his fun. Lord Rockwell obviously owed someone a great deal of money, or was in some form of trouble, but not with him, so Adam really couldn't care less.

"Are you musical, your Grace?" Lady Rockwell put in, leaning eagerly forward across her husband.

"I'm afraid not."

"Oh, what a pity! Olivia is so talented. You must hear her play."

"Mama, please!" Olivia demurred. Adam suspected that her modesty was as false as the rubies in her hair.

"We should hear her play." Evelyn said, as social cues dictated that she should. "Adam, go and turn the pages for her, won't you?"

Adam considered finding an excuse, but there really wasn't one. The pianoforte was opened, and Olivia took her seat. Her parents and Evelyn gathered at a respectful distance, and Adam took up his place at her side, ready to turn the pages.

He couldn't read music, which would likely be an issue, but Adam was finding it difficult to care.

Olivia started to play, the gentle music drowning out their conversation from the others.

"They want us to marry each other." She said brusquely.

Adam blinked, sure that he had misheard. "I beg your pardon?"

"I said, they want us to marry each other. Your mother, and my parents."

Well. What was a gentleman supposed to say to that? Adam shifted uncomfortably from foot to foot.

"Yes, I think they do."

Honesty seemed like the best policy. Olivia glanced briefly up at him.

"Well? Do you want to get married?"

Adam found himself floundering for words yet again.

"Well... I..."

"To me." She added. "I should have specified. Come, your Grace, it's a simple question. Do you want to get married to me? Yes, or no?"

"No."

"There, that wasn't so difficult, was it? Now we both know exactly where we are with each other, and there'll be no wasted time."

Adam coughed. "I see. You are remarkably straightforward, Miss Sixsmith."

She shrugged. "This is my third Season, and I need to get married. I want to get married, too. If I marry well, I'll be happy and settled. I'll have a family, hopefully, and I'll be able to get Papa out of whatever hole he's dug himself into this time. I don't know whether he owes you money..."

"He doesn't."

"Well, he owes somebody money. I know it's risky, being so frank like this, but you seem a decent sort of man, and it's not like anyone else can hear us."

"Don't you want to marry for..." Adam hesitated, feeling bewildered and half a step behind. "For love?" he finished, feeling silly.

Olivia shot him a look of disdain. "Page."

It took him a heartbeat to realize what she meant. He darted forward, turning the page, and the music continued.

"The older I get, the more I believe that love only exists between the pages of a novel." Olivia continued. "Romantic love, at least. My parents love me, and I love them, and I shall love whatever family I have. But marrying for love simply isn't practical. Not for people like us, your Grace. Gentlemen like you need an heir, and ladies like me need a comfortable home of our own. It's a transaction, pure and simple. Boiling a marriage down to its basic elements allows a person to make the most logical choice, for the best reasons."

"How very... practical of you."

Olivia flashed a grin up at him. "What are you thinking, your Grace? You look perplexed."

"I was wondering how on earth I could have thought you were a vacuous Society miss. You're one of the most shocking young ladies I've ever met."

"Hm. Well, unless you've changed your mind about marrying me – you are a spectacular catch, by the way – I really don't care what you think of me."

He gave a short laugh. "I hate being called a catch. It makes me feel like a fish. Still, I appreciate your honesty."

"You are quite welcome. I appreciate yours."

"I hope you find what you're looking for, Miss Sixsmith." Adam added, impulsively. He didn't feel drawn to Olivia, but she certainly seemed like the sort of person he would enjoy being friends with.

"Thank you. I hope you also find what you are looking for,

your Grace."

Adam cleared his throat, not sure why that statement had made him so uncomfortable.

"I'm actually not looking for anything."

The music finished with a flourish, and Olivia's hands fell still. Her doting parents broke into rapturous applause, and Evelyn into considerably more polite applause. Olivia looked up at Adam with a knowing look, one that seemed to see right through his forehead and into his brain. It was not a pleasant stare to receive.

"Oh, everyone is looking for something, your Grace. Much as you would like to be the exception, I am afraid that you are not."

Chapter Four

Chelwood Manor, Morning

Breakfast was already underway when Marina came stumbling down. She felt drained after last night.

Thankfully, Lord Ellersby wasn't able to request more than two dances, but he did his best to keep Marina busy all evening. He was an odious, insufferable man, but at least there was no danger of him appearing at the house with a bunch of flowers and that unpleasant smile. He'd told Marina last night, with more than a tinge of regret, that he had to leave on a business trip the following morning that would keep him occupied for some time.

Thank goodness for small mercies, Marina thought, smiling to herself. She felt good this morning. It was a new day, bright and fresh and clean, and the possibilities were endless.

She was being silly, feeling as though she'd only ever dance with gentlemen like Lord Ellersby. Why shouldn't things get better? She was barely twenty, she was pretty, and they were a rich, well-established family. She would be just fine.

"Morning, everyone." Marina said, slipping into the breakfast room and sitting down in her usual seat. They never ate in the cavernous dining room when it was just the four of them. Instead, they'd turned one of the parlours into a sweet little morning room, perfect for mealtimes. Some of the discarded garlands had been draped around the table, and Marina made a mental note to press some of the flowers for later, in her scrapbook.

Josephine was munching through a large bowl of porridge, listening avidly while Letitia recounted the events of last night. Samuel was staring at his untouched plate, his face white.

Marina hid a smile, remembering the impressive amounts of alcohol that Samuel had imbibed. He'd have to learn to slow down as he got older.

"... and Lady Woolfe said that the table decorations were quite the most beautiful thing she'd ever seen. Of course, her husband is a doctor, and he said..." Letitia babbled on and on, Josephine hanging on her every word.

Picking up a piece of toast, Marina began to butter it, only half listening to her mother.

"... and Lord Ellersby did monopolise Marina for most of the evening, but I'm sure that next time..."

"I can't take this anymore." Samuel burst out. He was still staring down at his plate, and his voice was thick with misery.

They all glanced at him, and Marina's gut clenched in warning. Something was wrong here, horribly wrong.

"Papa?" she managed, and Samuel finally dragged his eyes up from his plate. There was raw, naked despair in his face.

"I'm so sorry." Samuel whispered. "I've ruined everything. Everything."

Letitia cleared her throat. She'd gone white, but Marina noticed that she didn't look entirely surprised. She reached out, placing her hand on Samuel's where it lay on the table.

"Tell us, darling." She said quietly.

Samuel drew in a deep, ragged breath.

"Rina, Joey, I'm extremely for sorry over what this will do to you. You girls had such a bright future... oh, I've let you down so horribly."

"Papa? You're scaring me." Marina whispered. She still had a slice of bread in one hand, a butter knife poised in the other. It was as if she was frozen.

Samuel closed his eyes.

"Our finances have been... well, they'd been bad over the past few years. I like to play cards, girls, and I'm afraid that my habit has gotten rather out of hand."

"Oh, darling." Letitia murmured. This was clearly not news to her, although it certainly was to Marina.

"The business has not been doing well." Samuel pressed on, doggedly. "I had an idea for a new venture – more of the same, you know, breeding and selling horses – but I needed capital. I borrowed a large amount of money from a moneylender. The interest was high, but I was so sure of myself."

Marina knew where this was going. She felt dizzy and sick, all the food and alcohol from last night bubbling around in her gut, threatening to make a reappearance.

"It hasn't been going well. There's no money left of the investment." Samuel pressed on. "I... you don't know this, Letitia, my darling, but I thought I could win back the money to pay the loan. Oh, and the crippling interest. I wagered on horses, and played cards, and I was deeply, deeply unlucky."

Letitia went white. "Samuel?"

"It's all gone, every last penny. There's no more. I can't repay that outrageous moneylender, not if we sold every stick of furniture in the house."

"Samuel!" Letitia gasped. "Language! Not in front of the girls! Girls, out, now. Your father and I need to talk."

Marina and Josephine broke out into protests. It was unthinkable to be thrown out now, when all of this was happening. When their lives were about to change forever, and not for the better.

"No, let them stay." Samuel insisted. "This affects them too. Letitia, my love, I'm so sorry. I tried to hide it from you, I thought perhaps one more wager would recoup our losses, at least buy us some time..."

"You lost again, didn't you?" Letitia said, her voice flat.

The silence said it all.

Letitia drew in a shuddering breath and dropped her face into her hands.

"How long do we have?" she whispered. "Do we have any time at all?"

Samuel swallowed reflexively. "I don't know, but I can't even begin to pay what we – what I – owe. They'll strip the house down to the bare bones, then sell it, but that won't cover the debt. The interest alone will cripple us. I've run out of ideas."

"Why didn't you tell me this before that... that ridiculous party last night?" Letitia demanded.

Bile rose in Marina's throat. She remembered the expensive champagne, the flowers, the food, the cost of her own dress... everything had a price tag on it, and she'd wasted the hideously expensive night writhing in Lord Ellersby's company.

"I... I wanted us to have one last night together. One last party as a family. A last hurrah, I suppose." he answered lamely.

Anger flickered in Letitia's eyes. "That money I spent on the party. Did we have that money? I'm not asking if we could afford it. I know that we couldn't. I'm asking if we even had that much money. Half of it, even."

"Letitia..."

"The truth, Samuel, please. You've hidden enough from me. I want the truth, now."

He closed his eyes. "No."

She bit her lip, chin wobbling as if she were about to burst into tears.

"On the flowers alone, I spent... oh, I can't bear to think of it." Letitia whispered. "So wasteful. So silly."

"I'm sorry, darling. I... I've ruined everything. How you must all despise me." Samuel was on the brink of tears himself, water glistening in his eyes as he looked around the table. "Girls, I have betrayed you. I can't apologise enough, as words won't undo the harm I've done."

"It's alright, Papa." Josephine spoke up, her voice tremulous. "I'm sure we'll get through this."

"Yes, we will." Letitia agreed, reaching out to take Samuel's hand again. Anger and misery still shimmered in her eyes, but she still grabbed at her husband's hand like it was a lifeline. Their fingers twined together, squeezing tightly, hanging onto each other desperately. "We'll stick together as a family."

As a family. The words ran hollow. Marina knew what happened to debtors like her father.

Marshalsea. That was what happened to men like her father. It was an awful prison stuffed full of debtors, all rotting together, forgotten, until the debt could be paid. It was supposed to be a prison for other criminals too, of course, but at the moment, it was mostly populated with debtors. It was estimated that around two-thirds of the population was men and women who owed too much money to the wrong people. Poor debtors, who would never be able to repay what they owed.

The jailers were drunken, vicious louts, who could hurt prisoners any way they liked and get away with it. If a prisoner wanted their own cell – they were generally packed in five or seven to a room, at best – they had to pay a hefty bribe. Visitors needed to pay the guards, and if you sent in food or clothes for a prisoner, of course the guards would take it. And if a prisoner got on the wrong side of the guards – well, torture wasn't unheard of in that place. And if a prisoner even died, who cared?

Nobody, that's who.

There was one solution. Only one.

"I have to get married." Marina announced. "If I marry a rich man, our problems will be solved."

Letitia smiled tearfully at Marina. "You're such a sweet girl, Rina. So selfless. Isn't she, Samuel? Darling, this isn't what we wanted for you. This is not your knot to untie."

"You're a kind girl." Samuel agreed. "But I'm not sure we have time. The house and everything in it will be forfeited soon. I don't know how long we have, but news of my finances is starting to leak out. The moneylender is already starting to demand his money. He has a reputation."

"Couldn't you talk to him?" Josephine suggested, a touch of colour coming back to her cheeks. "If we could just explain, ask for more time..."

Samuel shook his head. "I know this man. He's merciless. He'll collect his money, no matter what. He's already sent members of the ton to Marshalsea, and he won't make an exception for me."

"I can marry a rich man who will solve our problems." Marina repeated.

Letitia shot her a pitying look. "Darling, you'd never find a man in time. There'd be no way to hide what's happening. He'd find out about our finances, and even if it still went ahead, then the engagement would take too long..."

"I can marry Lord Ellersby."

There was a little silence at this. Josephine, glanced from her father's face to her mother's, a faint crease on her otherwise smooth young brow.

"Who is Lord Ellersby? Rina? Who is he? You haven't mentioned him. Mama? Papa? Will somebody please tell me what's going on?"

"I won't let you marry that man." Letitia said, her voice quavering. "He might have bullied your father into letting him dance with you once or twice, but you will never marry him."

Marina swallowed hard. A lump had formed in her throat, like she'd swallowed something that wouldn't go down. She concentrated on keeping her face composed and her eyes free of tears. She needed to stay strong if she was going to carry through with her plan.

Please, Mama, don't weaken my resolve. Do you think I want to marry him?

"Lord Ellersby clearly likes me." Marina said firmly. "I don't... don't believe he's interested in my money. He has plenty of his own."

Letitia shook her head stoutly. "The man is a lecherous, drunken,
crawling..."

"He's rich." Marina interrupted. "Very rich. Rich enough to pay off your debts, isn't he, Papa?"

Samuel looked as though he was going to be sick.

"Yes." He whispered. "Yes, he could do that. And he would agree to marry you quickly. He likes you, and he's asked to marry you before. I said no. I said that he'd need to secure your consent, but if we told him that Marina changed her mind, he'd agree. He wouldn't mind if the marriage was... was more transactional. It might make some men uncomfortable, but not him."

"I don't like this." Josephine stated, wrapping her arms around herself. "Mama?"

Letitia was white, this time with anger.

"Samuel, am I to believe that you are seriously considering this idea? Considering giving – no, selling! – our daughter to this awful man? I am ashamed of you!"

"Don't be angry at Papa." Marina pleaded. "I don't like Lord Ellersby any more than you, but really, what choice do we have? What will happen to the three of us when Papa goes to Marshalsea? What about Josephine's coming-out? What about our futures? If I marry Lord Ellersby, I'll be a married woman, at least. I'll be comfortable. Papa will not go to prison, and Josephine will be able to go out into Society next year, as planned. Can't you see that this is the answer to our problems? Like Papa said, Lord Ellersby would marry me immediately. There's nothing else we can do."

"No, no, no." Letitia moaned, burying her face in her hands.

Samuel looked as if he were in pain. He leant forward across the table, hand stretching out for Marina's. He couldn't quite reach her outstretched hand, and it felt like a heavy-handed metaphor.

"Lord Ellersby is..." he paused, searching for the right word. "... is not a kind man. He has many, many flaws. He had an unpleasant past, which you would be advised not to dig into. Don't cross him, darling. Don't underestimate him. He is not a good man, do you understand?"

Marina nodded. "I understand, Papa. I know what I'm doing. I don't relish this any more than anyone else, but I don't believe that we have any other option. Will you speak to Lord Ellersby about this? Make it clear that it is a marriage of convenience. I doubt that he'd believe that I was in love with him, but I don't suppose he'd care if I didn't."

Samuel flinched at that, momentarily closing his eyes.

"My poor girl." He whispered. "What have I done? This is a wo

punishment than Marshalsea. If it wasn't for the fact you three would come to grief and a miserable end with me in prison, I should forbid the whole thing."

"But we will come to grief." Marina said quietly. "Won't we? We'll be out on the streets. None of our friends will help us. We need to keep you out of Marshalsea, Papa. At all costs. Will you speak to Lord Ellersby?"

Samuel nodded. "I will. He's away on business, but as soon as he returns, I shall speak to him about it. We can make the arrangements within a few days. It... it won't be a pretty wedding, my darling."

Marina lifted her chin. "I know, Papa. I know."

Letitia burst into noisy, uncontrollably tears. Marina, much to her own surprise, did not cry at all. Maybe all of her tears had already dried up.

Chapter Five

Contrary to popular opinion, Adam did not enjoy wringing money out of various whining noblemen. His father might have enjoyed making his debtors suffer, but Adam much preferred a nice, smooth transaction. It was not a complicated thing, this business of his.

At least, it shouldn't be.

The whole thing was shockingly simple. He lent money to men (and occasionally women, but less often) who needed it. A percentage of interest was agreed upon. Payments were made regularly, over an agreed-upon period of time, until the whole thing was paid off.

They borrowed. He lent. They paid. Simple.

In Adam's opinion, members of the ton were the worst. Of course, bad debts were a risk in every class of person, but logically the members of the ton should have been better equipped to pay back what they'd borrowed. They lived in palaces, after all, and dressed in silks, satins, and feathers. They dripped with jewels worth hundreds or even thousands of pounds. And, in the case of Samuel Cornish, Lord Chelwood, they also threw extravagant, expensive parties.

Adam had had enough. He wanted his money back, and he wanted it now. Lord Chelwood was in for a nasty shock if he thought Adam would simper and dance around the subject like the rest of the ton.

His carriage rattled up the drive towards Cornish House. It was a pretty place, although the gardens needed a little attention and the gravel needed raking. Adam's carriage needed restringing, actually, and so he'd been horribly bounced and jolted around on the way here, which wasn't improving his mood.

The carriage drew to a halt, and Adam jumped out with relief, stretching out his cramped limbs.

Now, he thought. To business.

He walked confidently up the stone steps — chipped and worn with use, he noted, and in need of a little sprucing up — and knocked smartly on the door with his cane.

Now for the hard part.

Getting inside.

A lock clicked, and the door opened, revealing a politely surprised butler.

"Good morning, sir." He said hesitantly.

"Duke of Brixham to see Lord Chelwood." Adam said brusquely, not bothering to offer a card.

The butler opened and closed his mouth, obviously thinking of something to say and deciding against it. The obvious question to ask was the polite but accusing: are you expected, your Grace?

But of course Adam was fixing him with an intent and disapproving glare, and the butler thought better of it.

"I'm sorry, your Grace, but his lordship is indisposed."

That, of course, would be the end of the matter in polite Society. Perhaps Adam might hum and haw, ultimately offering a card and requesting the Lord Chelwood repay the call at his earliest convenience.

Of course, Adam had no intention of doing that.

"Indisposed?" he echoed, disapproval hanging on his voice. "What do you mean, indisposed? This is a business matter, not a social call."

The butler flushed, but admirably stood his ground.

"His lordship is not seeing visitors at the moment." He said firmly, making as if to close the door in Adam's face.

Certainly not, Adam thought, with a rush of anger.

The butler was a tall man, taller than Adam, but thin, lanky, and elderly. It was an easy enough matter to shoulder past him and into the hall. It was an unexpected move, and the butler staggered back, unbalanced and shocked.

"Sir!" he shouted, forgetting his manners and Adam's title in one smooth move. "Sir, I must protest!"

"I won't be a moment." Adam replied, striding away down the hallway, cane clutched in one fist. He'd likely only have one chance to find Lord Chelwood's study, before the butler recovered his equilibrium and collected some burly footmen to throw him out.

Fortunately, all these grand houses were laid out in the same way.

Adam opened a door, and found himself in Lord Chelwood's study. The man himself was slumped forward over a desk, asleep and snoring, with a half-empty bottle of whiskey dropping from his nerveless fingers.

The butler was still puffing and panting after Adam down the hall, so he had a moment or two. Narrowing his eyes, Adam stepped forward. He brought the handle of his cane neatly down on the surface of the desk, only a few inches from Lord Chelwood's drooling face.

It made a tremendously satisfying bang. Lord Chelwood jolted awake with a squeal, his face reddened and creased from the papers lying underneath his head. His gaze was blurry and heavy with sleep, but he sobered up rapidly when he saw Adam.

The butler burst into the study behind him.

"Your Grace, I must protest!" he squawked. "Your lordship, I cannot

apologise enough. This gentlemen pushed past me. I shall have him removed at once."

Lord Chelwood glanced nervously up at Adam, who flashed him a distinctly predatory grin.

"I suppose you could have me removed, Lord Chelwood." Adam said, pleased at how low and menacing his voice sounded. "This is, after all, your house. For how much longer remains to be seen, of course."

Lord Chelwood swallowed reflexively, his double chin wobbling with fear.

"Nothing to worry about, Bennett. I... I do have an appointment with his Grace, I'd... I'd quite forgotten. A tray of tea would be nice, thank you."

The butler – Bennett – was clearly not convinced. Still, he pressed his thin lips together and made a half-hearted bow, withdrawing from the room and leaving the gentlemen alone. He closed the door behind him, and Lord Chelwood looked as though he wished he hadn't.

"You didn't have to scare poor Bennett like that." Lord Chelwood said, his voice small. "He's an excellent butler, and a very loyal one. I like him very much, we all do."

Adam snorted. "Well, you'll have to let him go soon enough, won't you?

Unless, of course, you have my money ready to pay me back."

He hooked the handle of his cane around the leg of a nearby chair, pulling it out from under the desk. He sat down with a flourish, glad that he'd remembered to bring his cane. It was a useful prop, even if he didn't actually use it for walking.

Lord Chelwood went white at the mention of money, as Adam had known he would.

"I... I will have your money very soon..."

"You know, I don't believe you. Samuel – may I call your Samuel? Your behaviour hasn't been very lordly, if you don't mind me saying – you have claimed to have my money more times than I can count over our period of business together. And yet, I have still not received my money."

Lord Chelwood now went red. It was impressive change of colours in such a short time, really.

"No, but this time I do mean it. I will have your money very soon. I really will, we've come up with a plan... oh, that doesn't matter. I will have your money. I just need a little while longer. A week, perhaps, or..."

"Would you prefer a month? Two months? A year, maybe?" Adam echoed, mocking. He leaned forward, resting his elbows on the desk. Lord Chelwood automatically leaned back, quailing.

"Do you know, Samuel, what annoys me the most about men like you?"

Lord Chelwood didn't ask what, but he swallowed hard and said nothing, so Adam continued.

"I buy debts from traders, you know. These traders let members of the ton – lords and ladies like yourself, dear sir – buy on credit. A mistake, I fancy, but of course it stands to reason that these fine people will be able to pay. Well, they can't. Or they don't. The traders send in bill after bill, coming politely and deferentially to their customers, asking to be repaid, and they are sent away with empty pockets and a flea in their ear. If I had a penny for every small trader that came into my office, unable to reclaim their fees from men like you, I would have a second fortune. Do you have any idea how

infuriating it is to meet modistes and tailors who can't pay their supplies
because the fine ladies and gentlemen they serve refuse to settle their bills? Grocers and butchers who'd supplied enough food to feed a thousand suddenly find themselves in debt, and Lord So-and-so bluntly tells them that he has no intention of paying."

"But I..."

"Don't interrupt. I even met a delightful middle-aged couple, who put all their savings into a house, which they allowed a lord and lady to rent from them. They served the said lord and lady, who they seemed to think were akin to gods. They gave them food, waited on them, served their guests, and so on. The rent was not paid. The rent was never paid. The lord and lady moved on without notice, leaving the couple on the brink of destitution. Do you think that is fair, Lord Chelwood?"

A vigorous shake of the head was his reply.

"What... what happened to the couple? The ones who were cheated out of rent, I mean." Lord Chelwood ventured.

Adam blinked, missing a beat. "I bought the debt from them, so they got their money back. Then I got my money back from the lord and lady. Well, some of it. The gentleman went to Marshalsea in the end."

Lord Chelwood shuddered at that word. Scenting blood, Adam pressed his advantage.

"So, Samuel, I'm sure you'll forgive me if I don't have any pity for you right now. I'm here for my money, or at least to see proof that you can pay."

Lord Chelwood swallowed hard again. "My... my oldest daughter is getting married. Her husband-to-be will pay."

Adam sighed. "Do you think I'm a fool? My patience has run out. I'm not waiting any longer."

The tubby, nervous man straightened his back just a little, a sure sign that he was about to gather his courage and say something. Interesting. Adam composed himself to wait.

"If you send me to Marshalsea, you won't get your money." Lord Chelwood said. His voice wobbled a little, but all in all, he spoke with an impressive amount of confidence. "However, if you're willing to wait a week, you'll get your money. In full. Plus interest."

"In a week's time you and your family might have absconded to France."

"How? We have no money!"

Adam shrugged. He was losing interest now. These confrontations were never as fun as he imagined in his head.

"Men like you always manage. And I think you've overlooked a crucial fact here."

"What?"

Adam leaned forward again, and Lord Chelwood shrank back into his chair. The whiskey was missing its cork, and the smell of alcohol was acrid and unpleasant in Adam's nose. That didn't help his temper.

"I don't care if I get my money."

Fear flashed across Lord Chelwood's face, plain and simple. "Your Grace, please. I have a family..."

That was the worst thing he could have said. Adam had heard variations of this excuse more times than he could possibly remember. He'd heard it from drunken men who beat their wives and children whenever they felt like it, and wasted their wages on drink and other women. He'd heard it from gawky young lords who believed they really were special and better than everyone else, married to dead-eyed Society Beauties who had no idea that life could be better than this.

In short, Adam had heard this excuse too many times to be moved in the slightest. And, of course, there was an obvious reply to this.

"If you care so much about your family, Lord Chelwood," Adam said softly, dropping the pretence at informality, "You ought to have thought about that before your gambled away their fortunes."

"I... I thought I could make things better." Lord Chelwood whispered.

Adam sat back in his seat with a sigh. He was getting tired of this conversation. It was going the same way as all the others were going - round and round in circles. Any pity he might once have felt was smothered under the sure knowledge that Lord Chelwood was no different from the rest. Thoughtless, entitled, spiteful. Angry and shocked when confronted with the consequences of his own actions. Adam resolutely didn't let himself think about the families. Sometimes they were complicit in their father, husband, or brother's mistakes, sometimes not. Either way, he couldn't allow the debtor to escape what he'd done just because he felt sorry for some poor woman and her children.

"You didn't make it better." Adam said tiredly. "You made it worse. I know everything, Lord Chelwood. I know that you wasted my money on a wager, and then you lost. Dramatically, I might add. It's not a surprise. Men and women who borrow money from me are not blessed with good luck."

"When my daughter is married…"

"I've heard no talk in town of your daughter's engagement. I don't take well to liars."

The man flushed. "I am not lying."

Adam inspected his nails. "And, as I said earlier, I don't believe you. Engagements aren't quiet things. They tend to be lengthy, too, which makes it unlikely that you'd have my money within a week, even if I were willing to wait that long."

"It's a rather sudden arrangement…"

"Do stop, Lord Chelwood. You're embarrassing us both."

As always, there was a limit to how much humiliation and flat, bland truth a man could make. Lord Chelwood appeared to have found his limit.

He reddened with anger, which didn't sit right on his good-natured face. Rising to his feet, Lord Chelwood leaned forward over his chest, hands splayed out for support. Adam resisted the urge to get to his feet, too. There was power in staying comfortably sitting while one's opponent fidgeted, standing in front of you like a supplicant.

"I will have that money in a week." He said, his plummy voice as forceful as he could make it go. "Plus the interest. In short, your Grace, you will be paid in full within a week. If you are not willing to wait a week, then I shall tell everyone in Society that you threw me into prison and my family out onto the street, over a matter of seven days. You already have a poisonous reputation, as I'm sure you're aware. I really don't think it would do you any good, especially considering my wife's popularity and my oldest daughter's fine success during the Season. Not to mention, of course, her fiancé, whose marriage to my daughter hinges on me not going into Marshalsea."

Adam let out a burst of laughter. "You're selling your own daughter to pay your debts? Good Lord, man, that's disgraceful. As to my reputation, I don't give a damn about it."

The oath echoed in the room, and Lord Chelwood flinched at the crudeness of the word. To his credit, he didn't cower away.

"You are a cruel man."

"So I've been told." Adam replied.

"They said your father was a cold-hearted, repulsive man, and you are his mirror image. I hope you're proud."

Adam was on his feet before he knew what he was doing. He fisted his hand in the frothy white lace of Lord Chelwood's cravat, hauling him forward over the desk until they were almost nose to nose.

The man gave a squeak of fright. Adam knew that his expression was twisted in an ugly way, lip curled and eyes blazing. There was a heartbeat, during which neither of them spoke.

No. I am not like him. I am not like him.

The thought echoed round and round in Adam's head, but the words wouldn't come out of his mouth. How could they? Lord Chelwood was unfailingly, infuriatingly right.

Then the man's gaze slipped over Adam's shoulder, and he sucked in a breath.

"Marina!" He gasped. "Leave, at once."

Adam glanced over his shoulder to see who was there.

A girl – no, a young woman – stood in the doorway. The door was open, and she hadn't made a sound. Her expression was calm and impassive, eyes fixed firmly on Adam.

"Who are you?" she said, her voice steady. "And more to the point, why do you have your hands on my father? If I were you, I should let him go at once."

Chapter Six

She was beautiful, that was for sure. Adam blinked at the woman, a little taken aback. This wouldn't be the first time he'd been accosted by relatives or friends of his debtors, but there was something about this woman that made him stop for a moment, carefully considering his next move.

Lord Chelwood gave a strangled squeak. "Marina, please! Don't talk to this man. He's a dangerous scoundrel."

The woman – Marina – barely glanced his way.

"Papa, I know what I'm doing."

Adam raised his eyebrows. He wasn't entirely convinced that she did, despite the self-assurance in her voice.

"I shouldn't talk to me like that, Miss…?"

"Lady Marina Cornish." She said sharply.

"Forgive me, Lady Marina. I am the Duke of Brixham, and I'm afraid to tell you that your dear papa owes me quite a bit of money. Money which I'm quite entitled to reclaim, despite his protests."

"Yes. I know. He'll have the money soon."

"He mentioned." Adam wavered, considering bringing up the subject of Lady Marina's upcoming marriage, but decided against it. It likely wasn't a pleasant subject, and something that put Lord Chelwood in a distinctly unflattering light.

"And you aren't willing to wait?"

"I'm not willing to trust that he really will have my money in a week's time. Unfortunately, I've heard all the excuses in the book, and most of them are nothing more than hot air."

Lady Marina pressed her lips together, gaze darting between her father and Adam. She was clearly thinking of what to do next, and that left Adam free to inspect her.

He knew of Lady Marina, in the same way he knew of the other young ladies and gentlemen of the ton. It was a chore, memorizing all the extensive families in Society, especially when they were all intermarried in the most inconvenient way. He knew that Lord Chelwood had two daughters, both unmarried, and Lady Marina was the only one Out. And this was her second Season, if he wasn't mistaken.

She was an exceptionally pretty young woman, in a thoughtful, sharp sort of way. She had light brown hair, pulled back in a messy, unfashionable style that suited her nonetheless. Her eyes were green – no, brown – or perhaps hazel. She had a delicate oval face and pale skin, and a way of looking a person directly and unapologetically in the face, which Adam found quite "refreshing. It was, after all, the fashion for ladies to be falsely modest, keeping their gazes levelled at the ground.

He hated that sort of affectation and was glad to see that Lady Marina didn't subscribe to that nonsense.

A moment too late, Adam realized that Lady Marina had noticed his scrutiny, and was staring back with a mixture of amusement and contempt.

"You still haven't released my papa." She said.

Adam let go of Lord Chelwood, who collapsed back into his seat with a muffled oof of surprise. He recovered quickly, scrambling to his feet and away from the desk, putting distance between himself and Adam.

"Marina, darling, you ought not to be here. His Grace is… ahem. I don't want you involved in this. Go find your mama and wait until I come out of the study."

Lady Marina pressed her lips together, gaze flashing over her father's form, looking for injuries.

"I'm not leaving you alone with this brute, Papa."

Once again, that was not the first time Adam had been called a brute, and the word had long since lost his sting.

Or so he'd thought.

For an instant, Adam saw himself through Lady's Marina's eyes. A grim, unforgiving man, willing to lay hands on a tubby, harmless gentleman like Lord Chelwood, rude and unkind.

He gave himself a little shake, reminding himself that he was well within his rights to be here and demand his money. As always, Adam conjured to mind the image of various desperate traders, unable to demand back their money from their illustrious, titled debtors.

Thus fortified, Adam spoke.

"You can call me whatever names you like, Lady Marina, but the simple fact is that your papa owes me money. I am well within my legal right to demand my money back."

"You aren't a poor man." She retorted. "You don't need that money. What about the moral right of the thing?"

Adam snorted. "What about the poor traders who go into debt because men like your papa don't feel as though they need to pay their bills? What about them?"

Lady Marina blinked at that. "We don't owe any traders money. Do we, Papa?"

Lord Chelwood shook his head. "Marina, please. Let us talk in private."

"No. This man is violent, Papa. He could have seriously hurt you."

Adam rolled his eyes. "For crying out loud."

"What am I to think about it, then?" she snapped. "I heard raised voices, and came in here to find you manhandling my poor father. How can you explain that?"

Adam spread his hands apart. "A momentary lapse of temper, for which I apologise. It won't happen again. The next time anyone will lay hands on your papa will be when the bailiffs come to escort him to Marshalsea."

That word had the intended effect. The colour drained from Lady Marina's face.

"You can't do that."

"I can, and I will. I'm sorry, Lady Marina. Even if I wished to make an exception for your papa, I couldn't. The rest of the ton would demand that I make an exception for them too, and they are noticeably less deserving."

Lady Marina swallowed hard, glancing over her father. Adam saw a flash of fear on her face. Not fear for herself as such, but for her father. And well might she be afraid. Marshalsea was an awful place, and a man like Lord Chelwood wouldn't last long. A pang of pity ran through Adam's chest, hastily smothered. His business didn't allow for pity, not even a drop.

"You really won't wait a week?" Lady Marina said, her voice so quiet he almost didn't hear her.

Adam fidgeted, not wanting to look at the agonized expression on Lord Chelwood's face. This meeting wasn't going at all how he planned.

"Business is business, Lady Marina." He muttered. "You shouldn't have to concern yourself with this."

She snapped her gaze back to him, piercing and unblinking.

"I would do anything to save my father, your Grace. Anything at all."

Adam remembered the marriage that Lord Chelwood had mentioned, the poorly disguised business deal involving Lady Marina herself, and realized for the first time that she'd entered into it willingly.

Poor girl. She deserved a better father, really, and he couldn't have chosen a better daughter.

Keep your emotions out of it, boy, the old Duke's voice echoed in his head, disdainful and angry. Emotion never got anyone anywhere. Plain, good sense and business dealings, that's what you want.

Adam cleared his throat, pushing back his shoulders.

"Lady Marina, I really would like to talk to your father in private, if you wouldn't mind."

"Yes, Marina, please leave." Lord Chelwood seconded eagerly. The humiliation was probably getting too much.

Lady Marina didn't leave. Really, Adam hadn't expected her to. She was still staring at him with that unwavering stare, which had taken a decidedly calculating turn.

"I've heard all about you, your Grace." She said, her voice almost menacing.

"Oh, I'm sure you have."

She gave her head a brief shake. "Not the money-lending business, as unpleasant as that is. I hear that you're looking for a wife."

Adam flinched. That was not the direction he'd thought this

conversation would go.

"I beg your pardon?"

"You need to get married and produce an heir." Lady Marina ploughed on, ignoring the agonized looks Lord Chelwood kept shooting her. "But, of course, none of the suitable young ladies will have you."

Adam narrowed his eyes. "I think you're talking about something you don't understand, Lady Marina."

"Oh, but I do understand. You're a notorious money-lender, which is far beneath your dignity as a nobleman, not to mention the lengths you'll go to get back your money. The rest of the ton are afraid of you, certainly, but they also despise you. I daresay you don't care about that..."

"I certainly do not."

"... but now you're considering marriage. It must be a lonely life. Do you even have any friends, your Grace?"

Adam took a step forward, and Lady Marina didn't even flinch.

"How dare you speak to me like that?" he hissed.

She shrugged. "You don't scare me, your Grace. I don't owe you money. But I imagine that you're starting to panic, now. If you don't produce an heir, your title will go to some distant cousin, and your legacy forgotten forever. The Brixham estate will be torn into shreds, gone without a trace, almost. There would be plenty of people glad to see that happen, don't you think? And, of course, in your declining years, you'll have plenty of time to sit around, thinking of what will happen when you die, all alone and wishing things had worked out differently. I'm sure you've imagined it many times."

Adam had, but there was no way he would admit that here and now. He didn't like this sensation of fear and vulnerability. He didn't like how Lady Marina's sharp, unblinking eyes were looking straight through him, into him, entirely fearless and terrifyingly accurate.

"Madam, I suggest you watch your tone. I can have your papa..."

"Thrown into Marshalsea. Yes, I know, you have already said that.." Lady Marina interrupted with a careless wave of her hand.

Lord Chelwood had gone an interesting shade of purple. Adam wondered, in a careless sort of way, whether he would faint or not.

How could Lady Marina possibly know about this? Adam thought he'd been subtle in his search for a prospective duchess. He had wealth on his side, as well as breeding, and he wasn't an unattractive man. His youth was running out, though, and there was no denying the way his father's reputation overshadowed it all.

It was humiliating, watching ladies and gentlemen whisk away their daughters from before him as quickly as possible. There weren't many single ladies willing to converse with Adam in any case, and he wasn't about to embarrass himself by trying too hard. Olivia might have married him, but she seemed different to the other ladies in the ton. Besides, that didn't seem right, and he'd told her no. So, now what?

"You can throw Papa into jail," Lady Marina continued, eyes still fixed on Adam's face, "But that won't do anything about your problem, now, will it? You'll still be a single man, with no prospects of marriage unless you lower your standards significantly. Perhaps you know a maid who might marry you? A grocer's daughter, perhaps?"

Adam sucked in a breath at the insult, and Lord Chelwood gave a faint moan.

"What exactly is your point, Lady Marina."

She took a step closer, and Adam found himself retreating.

"You need to get married. You need an heir, but none of the ton would allow you to marry their daughters."

"So?"

"So, I will marry you."

There was a long, tense pause. Adam thought that he must have misheard.

"What did you say?" he managed eventually,

Lady Marina tilted back her head, no trace of shame in her face.

"I will marry you, your Grace, in exchange for you writing off my father's debt."

No, he had not misheard. Adam stared at her for a long moment, not sure if he should be amused or offended.

"You're mad." He glanced at Lord Chelwood. "She's mad."

Lord Chelwood seemed to come to life. He sprang in front of Lady Marina as if to defend her, for all the world as if it had been Adam who was proposing her.

"I won't have this sort of talk. Not in my house – and it is still my house, your Grace, at least for now – and not in my study. You mustn't talk like this, Marina. It is offence to the duke, and shocking to me. That's quite enough, do you hear?"

Lady Marina did not seem to be listening to her father. Her gaze was fixed on Adam's face, and to his own horror, he couldn't tear his eyes away.

Would it be the worst thing in the world?

Lady Marina obviously had nothing but contempt for him, but perhaps he would be a better choice than whatever awful man her dearest papa had picked out for her to marry. It would cut out the middleman, too.

If she'd liked the man she was meant to marry, she wouldn't have proposed to marry Adam so bluntly.

Adam chewed his lip, flicking over the facts and his own options. He could laugh in her face and leave and send in the bailiffs tomorrow. But then he would never get his money, not even once the house and everything in it was sold. And Lady Marina was right, too. Every member of the ton he sent to jail put him further and further away from marrying.

He would have liked to marry someone who impressed him at least. Adam wasn't a romantic, but the idea of a loving wife was alluring.

Lady Marina was... well, it was hard to describe what she was. Something about her interested him, even the straight, unafraid stare she was directing his way. Something clenched in Adam's chest, and he began to realize that marrying Lady Marina was more than interesting.

Lord Chelwood stood on his tiptoes, trying to put his face between Adam and Lady Marina's gaze. He was still trying to protect his daughter, although rather ineffectually.

Lady Marina didn't seem to have blinked at all.

"Well, your Grace?" she said, her voice cool and self-assured. "A simple yes or no will do."

"Marina!"

"Perhaps it isn't such a bad idea." Adam murmured.

Lady Marina was neither shocked nor pleased. She only raised her eyebrows.

"Yes, I know it isn't a bad idea. That's why I suggested it."

Chapter Seven

What are you doing? What are you doing? What are you doing?

The little voice in the back of Marina's mind was going wild, frantic. It demanded, over and over again, to know what on earth she thought she was getting herself into, and Marina did not have the answer.

In her mind, she wondered whether Samuel would call this a bluff, if they were playing cards. No, not a bluff, not that. For some reason, Marina kept thinking of a game of chess, and imagining that she was sacrificing her queen.

Well, that would be suicide in a game of chess. The queen was the most powerful piece on the board, and without it, the game was all but lost.

She didn't let any of this show on her face. At least, Marina hoped that she wasn't letting it show on her face. Samuel had told her once that she had a very good poker face, and she could only pray that he hadn't just been flattering her unnecessarily.

The Duke of Brixham had not been what she had expected. She'd heard his name before, of course, and it made sense that this was the merciless moneylender who had her poor papa over a barrel. But he didn't look at all like what Marina had imagined.

He was a well-built young man, somewhere in his mid-twenties but not yet near thirty, with a pair of broad shoulders, a full head of dark hair, and shimmering, icy-blue eyes that never seemed to blink.

He was handsome, and that didn't feel right. Weren't loathsome men supposed to be ugly, or at least horribly unpleasant, like Lord Ellersby?

Thoughts of Lord Ellersby propelled Marina on with her shocking, unladylike proposal. She didn't like the Duke, not one bit, but he was almost certainly a better option than Lord Ellersby. And, of course, he had the power to cancel out Samuel's debt. There was always the chance that Lord Ellersby would utilize some fancy financial footwork and manage to marry Marina without paying off Samuel's debt, and that would be horrifying. Marina didn't know how she would go on if that happened. Married to

Lord Ellersby, and her papa in Marshalsea.

No, this was a safer option by far, and at least the Duke was nicer to look at than Lord Ellersby, not that it counted for much.

The Duke was staring at Marina, as if he couldn't decide whether to storm out or... well, accept her proposal.

No, that couldn't be right. Marina's proposal was a long shot to say the least. Could she actually pull this off? Did she want to pull this off?

She wasn't sure that she liked the way the Duke was looking at her. It wasn't the hungry leer that Lord Ellersby levelled her way, or even a speculative, mildly interested look that she'd seen on various gentlemen before.

This was something different. Something sharp and curious.

"Perhaps it isn't such a bad idea."

Marina didn't know how to react. She hadn't expected that response, not right away. Careful to hide her surprise, Marina replied calmly.

"Yes, I know it isn't a bad idea. That's why I suggested it."

Samuel gave a stifled moan. Marina glanced at her father, and suppressed her panic at his expression. He looked as though he were going to be sick, although perhaps the almost-empty whiskey bottle on his desk could be to blame for that.

At least he had the sense not to openly forbid Marina's suggestion. Returning her gaze to the Duke, Marina waited for him to speak again. His gaze narrowed, but he kept the distance between them, making no move to come towards her.

"You understand that if we were to go ahead with your suggestion, your Papa's debt wouldn't be cancelled until we are actually wed."

"Yes, I understand. Still, better you than Lord Ellersby. I assume you're a man of your word."

The Duke rolled his eyes. "I am, but even if I wasn't, a man can't put his own father-in-law in debtor's prison, can he?"

Marina bit down on a sharp retort that perhaps he could. The Duke sighed, raking a hand through his hair. It was a strangely young gesture, and with his hair all dishevelled, he looked... well, he looked vulnerable. Marina's heart skipped a beat, and she scolded herself for it. He was the lesser of two evils, that was all.

"We will discuss this later." The Duke said briskly, glowering at Samuel. "I'll let you sober up, Lord Chelwood, then we can iron out the finer details at a later date. If I hear a whiff of Lady Marina getting engaged to anyone else, your debt will be payable in that very hour, do you understand? I don't intend for you to use this idea as leverage to gain more time."

Samuel swallowed hard, jowls wobbling as he composed a reply. Marina answered for him.

"We understand, your Grace."

"Very good. Good day to you both."

And just like that, the Duke strode out of the room, leaving the door swinging open behind him. Marina heard his footsteps recede down the hall, and the front door slammed. She let out a breath she didn't know she'd been holding, and Samuel sank down onto the seat behind his desk.

"Marina," he moaned. "What have you done? What are you thinking?"

Marina crouched down beside her father, who was worryingly pale by now. His hands were shaking, and she took one of them in her own.

"He's the lesser of two evils, Papa. Don't you think?"

"I don't think so, at all! The man is awful, everyone says so."

"Well, if he's an awful man, so is Lord Ellersby. If I'm to marry one of them, I might as well be a duchess. Besides, the Duke is much nicer to look at."

Samuel groaned. "Please don't tell me you've been taken in by a handsome face."

"Do you really think I would, Papa? Look, I can't bear the thought of marrying Lord Ellersby. I only suggested it because I wasn't about to let you go to Marshalsea. But now I have another option, and that's to marry the Duke. Given the choice, I truly feel as if the Duke is the best option for me. And he's all but agreed to it! Your debt will be written off immediately, and you won't have Lord Ellersby as a son-in-law. More to the point, I won't have him as a husband. Think about it, Papa."

Samuel nibbled at his lower lip, considering. The meeting had wrung the spirit out of him. Marina wasn't sure whether she wanted to throttle the Duke for frightening her father so badly or kiss him for offering her another way out of this awful mess.

"This is all my fault." Samuel said, his voice cracking.

"Papa, no..."

"No, Marina, don't comfort me. There's no way of looking at this which absolves me. I have done this. I risked your future, as well as your Mama's and Josephine's, all because of my own stupidity and carelessness. How could I have been so foolish? I'll never forgive myself, and you ought not to forgive me, either. What sort of father am I?"

Marina clutched at his hand. "Papa, stop. You've made a mistake – several, I must say – but that doesn't mean that we don't love you, and it doesn't mean that you don't love us. We'll get through this, and if I'm a duchess at the end of it, so much the better.

Marina continued talking, her voice a rhythmic, soothing thing in the quiet study. Samuel began to relax a little, listening to his daughter and thinking over what had just happened.

For her own part, Marina could barely process what she'd just done. She hadn't come here with the intent to offer herself as a wife to her father's creditor. She'd heard angry voices and came running in time to see the Duke of Brixham hauling Samuel forward over the desk. Anger had done the rest. She didn't know where the suggestion had come from, but a marriage of convenience didn't seem too shocking to the Duke. After all, Samuel's debts weren't well-known. If they guarded their secret well, the world might never know of the circumstances surrounding their marriage.

Marina was no duchess-in-waiting, but she had good breeding, a pretty face, and was well-liked in Society. As a match for the Duke of Brixham, she might not be his social equal, but in every other respect she would be considered an excellent match. The Duke was considered an unpleasant yet wealthy and powerful man, whereas Marina and her family were well-known and well liked.

In short, the Duke would benefit from the marriage almost as much as Marina and her family would benefit.

He's a clever man, Marina thought. He'll see the benefits for himself.

A part of her – a tiny, fluttering part deep inside – was excited to become a duchess. Not just any duchess – his Duchess. There was something interesting about the Duke, something exciting and attractive, and Marina was frankly surprised that more ladies hadn't noticed it.

Focus, Marina, she scolded herself. It's not arranged yet. The Duke might still change his mind, and then where will you be?

"Papa?" a small voice came from the doorway. Samuel seemed to be wrapped up in his own personal world of misery, and Marina glanced up instead.

Josephine stood there, white-faced, with her mother hovering behind.

"We heard voices." Letitia said, her voice trembling ever so slightly. "Angry voices. Was that him, Samuel? The man you owe money to?"

Samuel swallowed hard, forcing himself to look up and meet his wife's eyes.

"Yes, darling, that was him."

"He's younger than I thought he would be." Josephine chipped in.

"Yes, surely he might listen to reason..." Letitia began, without much hope.

Samuel shook his head, although there was a light in his eyes that wasn't there before.

"He won't be moved to let us off, darling, although perhaps... perhaps..."

He trailed off, and it was apparent to Marina that she would have to explain all this.

Sucking in a breath, she got to her feet, smoothing out her skirts.

"Mama, Josephine, there might be a change of plans. I think I am now marrying the Duke of Brixham instead."

There was a little silence.

"I beg your pardon?" Letitia managed. "What are you saying, Marina?"

"I am saying that the Duke needs a wife. Obviously, no self-respecting member of the ton would allow their daughters or sisters to marry a man who puts noblemen in gaol, so his options are rather limited. He needs a wife and he needs an heir, so I proposed a marriage of convenience in exchange for Papa's debts being written off."

A longer silence descended.

"You proposed?" Letitia squawked. "Oh, Marina..."

"He is better looking than Lord Ellersby though." Josephine pointed out, and some of the colour returned to Letitia's face.

"Well, he is a better match than him..." she murmured. "Samuel, what do you say to this?"

"I didn't say much." Samuel admitted. "Marina and the Duke mostly arranged it between them. She's a decent match for him."

"He's a duke." Josephine pointed out, snorting. "And Marina's pretty, but not that pretty."

Marina rolled her eyes at her sister's unfailing sisterly kindness.

"Thank you, Josephine. That's very nice."

Letitia strode into the room, arms folded, brow furrowed.

"And this is all sorted, is it? It's definite? The engagement is going ahead?"

Samuel shrugged. "It's hard to say. I would say... I might say so, yes. The Duke seemed interested, but of course you can never tell with a man like that. Oh, Lettie, I've made such a mess of this. I should be the one coming up with solutions, I should be the one dealing with this, not our lovely Marina."

"Papa, stop." Marina said. She felt drained, as though she'd run round and round the grounds at full speed, instead of engaging in one conversation with a strangely compelling man that she ought to dislike. She was running out of patience for her papa. It wasn't as if there was any other option for them, was there?

"I have to marry either the Duke or Lord Ellersby if we want to keep Papa out of Marshalsea." Marina continued tiredly. "And if I have the choice – which I'd very much like to have – I would rather marry the Duke for many different reasons."

"But what about..." Letitia began, but Marina held up a hand, shaking her head.

"Mama, please. I don't want to talk about this at the moment. I'm tired, and I feel a little shaky, so I might actually faint, even though I'm not a fainting sort of lady."

"You ought to sit down." Josephine suggested, more interested at the prospect of witnessing a swoon than sympathetic at her sister's plight.

Marina stuck out her tongue at her sister. "I think I'll go and lie down. Papa, if the Duke writes to you or sends any sort of message, I'd like you to tell me first. Would you mind doing that? It is me who's getting married, after all."

Samuel nodded. "Of course. Of course."

Marina pushed past her mother and sister, stepping out into the hallway. While her future was murky and unsure, she felt as though a great weight had been lifted off her shoulders. She wouldn't have to marry Lord Ellersby after all.

Would the Duke of Brixham be any better? Well, that remained to be seen.

Chapter Eight

The carriage ride home from Chelwood Manor was a very different affair from the carriage ride to the Manor. Adam sat numbly, staring into space and trying to wrap his head around what had just happened.

Was that an engagement? Was he engaged to Lady Marina? Possibly. It was hard to say.

Adam tried his best to unearth his emotions from the deep grave where he'd buried them – or rather, where the old Duke had insisted they be buried – and therefore decide how he felt about all this.

Conflicted. That was the answer he came up with. Conflicted.

Lady Marina did not want to marry him. Of course she didn't. Why would she? He was all but holding her father to ransom. The arrangement was something Adam would never, ever have suggested himself, but now that she had suggested it, he had to admit to feeling... well, excited. Intrigued. As if there was a brighter future beckoning him forward.

He shifted uncomfortably in his seat, reminding himself that the Cornish family were very much trapped upriver without any oars, and this was not a love match, not by any stretch of the imagination.

Who was she supposed to marry? She'd let slip a name – Lord Ellersby, that was it. Adam frowned, his brow scrunching up. Now, he knew him. He was an awful man, and explained perfectly why Lady Marina was happy to marry someone else – anyone else – who wasn't Lord Ellersby.

I'd be a better husband than him, Adam thought sourly. But then, so would half of England. The man's lecherous, and extremely unpleasant. What was Lord Chelwood about, letting his daughter enter into an arrangement with a man like that?

The answer presented itself at once, in the form of Lady Marina herself. She stood in Adam's imagination, back straight, chin high, gaze unwavering. She loved her father. That was apparent every time she looked his way. The man had let her down, and no mistake, but Lady Marina loved him nonetheless.

She would do anything to keep him safe, and there was the answer.

No doubt she'd fixed on marrying Lord Ellersby as the only way to pay off her father's debts, but Adam was the ideal solution. Why not deal with the problem at the source, after all?

The carriage turned into the drive leading up to Adam's home, and he leaned back in his seat, suddenly drained. It had been an exhausting day, and he'd somehow come out of it with an engagement.

It would solve his problems, though. It would be nice to have a wife. Lady Marina seemed like good company – somebody he could respect and even admire. Perhaps they would become friends. Perhaps, in time, they might even… no, that was too far. Adam carefully ended that train of thought, not wanting to engage in more romantic thoughts. There had seemed to be something between him and Lady Marina – or was that his imagination? It might well be his imagination. He ought not to require more of her than she was willing to give.

Marriage, though, Adam thought, with mingled panic and fascination. *I'm getting married.*

The carriage lurched to a stop, and Adam climbed out, still wrapped up in his own thoughts. If he planned to marry Lady Marina, he'd have to make his decision soon.

I didn't exactly say yes, he reminded himself. *But I didn't say no, either. Do I want to say no? Wouldn't it be easier if I just married her? Then Mother would stop nagging me.*

On cue, the door to the parlour opened, and Evelyn peered out.

"Ah, there you are, Adam. Come on in, I want to talk to you."

Adam thought wistfully of the piles of papers waiting for him in his study, along with the ever-patient and ever-menacing Matthew, but of course Evelyn wouldn't be denied. She'd already disappeared back into the parlour, with no doubt in her mind that Adam was following.

He handed his cane, hat, and coat to the footman, and followed his mother into the parlour.

She'd clearly been busy at her writing-desk. There were invitations and half-written replies scattered over the desk, and one particular invitation jumped out to Adam at once.

It was printed in gold writing on thick, creamy paper.

Lord and Lady Rockwell Request the Pleasure of your Company at a Small, Informal Soiree.

The date was written below. It was scheduled two days from now, indicating that Lord and Lady Rockwell had arranged it in a hurry.

That, in turn, indicated that they had ulterior motives. Adam could guess at those motives.

"Look." Evelyn said, beaming, swiping up the Rockwell invitation. "John and Susannah have invited us over. She sent me a little note along with it. It really is an informal little gathering – just us, the three of them, and possibly one or two other close friends. Won't that be nice? It was all a bit sudden, but they felt as though we all got along marvellously."

Adam sighed. "And will Olivia be there?"

Evelyn blinked. "Well, of course she will. It's her house. Don't think I didn't notice you and her getting along famously last time we all met up. Aren't you excited to see her again?"

"Mother, I can't remember the last time I was excited about anything. And while me and Olivia did get on, I'm not a fool. This is the prelude to courtship."

Evelyn flushed, telling Adam that he was exactly right.

"Well, so what if it is? She's a lovely girl."

"Indeed she is, but I don't want to marry her."

"Why not? Oh, Adam, I can't work you out at all. Olivia is pretty, clever, and interesting. Why wouldn't you want to marry her?"

Because Olivia doesn't have that strange, alluring fire that I saw in Lady Marina, Adam realized. Because there was something between me and Lady Marina in that study – on my side, at least – that was like a magnet pulling us together. I don't know what on earth is going on, but I intend to find out.

"Because I am engaged to Lady Marina Cornish." Adam said.

There was a long, fraught silence. Evelyn stared up at her son, frowning as if trying to make sense of what he'd said.

"Engaged?" she repeated. "To... to Lady Marina Cornish?"

"The very same."

Evelyn made a little fluttering motion with her hands and sat down heavily on the sofa. She'd gone pale, and Adam felt a twinge of guilt. Should he have broken the news more gently? Should he at least explain? Adam found that he wasn't keen to outline the circumstances of their engagement, but how would he avoid it? Evelyn wouldn't be pleased. Not one bit.

"How long have you been engaged?" Evelyn managed, keeping her voice tolerably calm.

"Oh, about an hour. Perhaps less. It was a tentative arrangement, but..."

"Tentative? Oh, for pity's sake, break it off, then! Olivia Sixsmith is a much better match."

"I don't want to marry Olivia, and she doesn't want to marry me. That is, she doesn't much mind whether she marries me or someone else."

"And Marina Cornish is head over heels for you, is she?" Evelyn withdrew a handkerchief, twisting it into knots in her hands. She glanced sharply at Adam, and he was uncomfortably aware that he probably looked guilty.

"There's something you're not telling me, Adam. I know you haven't been courting this girl, so explain why you're suddenly engaged to her. Explain yourself. At once."

"Mother..."

"At once!"

"The truth is that it's a marriage of convenience." Adam drew in a deep, fortifying breath. This explanation would not paint him in a good light. "Lord Chelwood, Marina's father, owes me a great deal of money. He can't repay it. His only hope is to marry off his daughter to someone rich enough to pay his debts for him."

Evelyn turned a worrying shade of purple. "He sold his daughter. To you?"

"No, not me, actually. To Lord Ellersby."

Evelyn wrinkled her nose. "Ugh, that awful man? Disgusting."

"I tend to agree. Lady Marina was the one who proposed cutting out the middleman and directly marrying me herself."

"To which you, as a gentleman, declined her desperate offer and instead offered to simply cancel the debt, yes? Please, Adam, tell me that this is how the story ends."

Adam bit his lip, avoiding his mother's gaze. "I can't just cancel his debt, Mother. You know that."

"That sounds like something your father would say." Evelyn responded coldly. Adam flinched. It was not a compliment. It was never a compliment.

"Look, Mother, you wanted me to get married, didn't you? Lady Marina will be a duchess. She proposed the marriage, not me."

"Oh, so she's vulgar and too forward then, is she? This is getting worse and worse, Adam."

He looked away, watching birds flit in front of the parlour window. They were always in pairs at this time of year. A pang of loneliness went through Adam's chest, hastily smothered. The old Duke had no truck with anyone who didn't relish being alone. He'd drummed it into Adam from a young age that people were not reliable, and their company should really be avoided by any sensible gentleman.

Looking back now, Adam couldn't help but wonder whether that was bitterness on his father's part. Not that it mattered. It was too late for Adam to change his ways, anyway.

Unless he married a woman who brought out the best in him. Someone who would stand up to him, challenge him, make him earn her respect, and earn his in return.

Maybe. Maybe not. But the fact remained that Adam's mind was made up.

"I'm going to marry her, Mother." Adam said briskly, turning away. "I'm sorry that I won't be marrying Olivia. I think I'll be too busy to attend Lord and Lady Rockwell's soiree. However, since news of my engagement will be around by then, I can't imagine they'll really be that happy to see me."

Evelyn looked away, her face taut. Disappointed.

"As you like, Adam. I hope you know what you're doing."

So do I, Adam thought, careful not to say it aloud.

***

To Lord Samuel Cornish, Earl of Chelwood

My good sir, I am writing to you in response to our conversation earlier today. This regards Lady Marina's proposal. I have thought carefully on the subject and have decided that the marriage should go ahead.

From this moment, I consider myself and Lady Marina to be an engaged couple. A common marriage license has been procured by me only this afternoon, and the marriage will take place in three days' time. I shall also send a brief missive to Lady Marina herself, informing her of this decision, and shall await her confirmation as well as yours.

Your debt has at this moment been frozen and will be cancelled altogether on the date of our wedding, once the ceremony has been completed. My steward will carry out the arrangements. If the marriage is cancelled beforehand, or for any reason does not go forward (barring obvious and unavoidable delays, of course), the debt will be unfrozen and payable immediately.

On a more a personal note, I would much prefer a very small wedding. On my side, only my mother will be attending. We can discuss this further, but the marriage must be carried out in three days' time, unless we all three agree otherwise. That is, myself, yourself, and Lady Marina.

I await your response.

Your obedient servant,

Lord Adam Blackburn, Duke of Brixham

Adam sent off the letter at once, and sat at his desk, eyeing the adjusted accounts book (adjusted to show Lord Chelwood's frozen debt amount) until the response came.

It came quickly and was sloppily written and brief.

Your Grace,

All of the conditions you have outlined are quite acceptable to both myself and my daughter. Marina has received your note and will include her signature at the bottom of my letter to indicate her agreement. Three days is entirely sufficient, and a very small wedding is acceptable to us.

Your obedient servant,

Lord Samuel Cornish, Earl of Chelwood, and Lady Marina Cornish

Well. That was that, then. Adam read over the letter several times, trying to understand the niggling disappointment he felt that Lady Marina hadn't written to him herself.

Resignation and misery reeked from Lord Chelwood's letter. Adam had read many letters from men at the end of their tether, with their spirit broken and the fight entirely gone out of them.

Any pity he might have felt was overshadowed by the spectre of the old Duke, grim and unforgiving. The old Duke never felt pity for anyone, not even his own son.

Adam placed Lord Chelwood's letter carefully on the desk, leaning back in his chair and regarding it. There was a blotchy mark on the corner of the paper, which could have been a drop of water, or perhaps a tear. He liked to think that it wasn't a tear.

She suggested it, Adam reminded himself. I need a wife, and her father needs his debt cancelled. I'll be better than Lord Ellersby, at least.

He kept coming back to that thought, since it was an irrefutable point. He would be a better husband than Lord Ellersby. He was the lesser of two evils, and that was something, at least.

Lady Marina's face kept darting up behind Adam's lids whenever he closed his eyes, hazel eyes unblinking and mesmerizing.

The gong rang from dinner, although Adam didn't feel much like eating. His mother had informed him that she would not be joining him.

She's angry at me, Adam thought tiredly. I've disappointed my only living parent. How wonderful.

Chapter Nine

Two Days Later

Marina couldn't sleep. That was hardly surprising, considering the fact her wedding was taking place tomorrow.

My wedding, she thought, a mixture of fear and anticipation springing up in her chest. She hadn't seen the Duke since the proposal – if it could be called a proposal – although he had, of course, sent her a letter.

That letter sat open on Marina's desk. She'd read it over several times, but hadn't replied. There didn't seem to be much to say.

She almost knew the contents off by heart, and they hadn't been what she was expecting at all.

To Lady Marina Cornish

I am writing to you to confirm your approval for our marriage. I have written to your father to confirm the date – three days from now – but I also wanted to communicate with you personally.

I know why you are doing this. To save your father, which is truly admirable. However, I want to be sure that this is your choice, and yours alone. If your father is using you as a pawn in his attempt to pay off his debt, I should like to know from you, as soon as possible. I don't believe that he is, but still.

I know you are not in love with me. This is of course a marriage of convenience, but I am keen that it should be – well, convenient for us both. I believe that you'll make a fine duchess, and I have no intentions of restricting your freedom once we are married.

You seem to be a courageous and intelligent young woman, and I hope we will get along very well together.

Yours,
Lord Adam Blackburn, Duke of Brixham

She hadn't replied. She ought to have, but it was easier to just sign her name at the bottom of Samuel's letter.

I believe you'll make a fine duchess.

Those words rang out in Marina's head, a little compliment that made her happier than it ought to do.

Not that it meant anything. She didn't know any more about the Duke today, on the eve of her wedding, than when she'd first burst into the study to find him standing there.

He might be worse than Lord Ellersby, Marina thought. She knew that a handsome face and a nicely worded letter didn't make a good man. The fact was that she knew nothing about the Duke of Brixham, and yet she was going to marry him anyway.

Supper had been a quiet, miserable affair. Letitia kept wiping away tears, and Samuel stared down at his plate, eating nothing. Marina felt, conversely enough, that she was somehow in the wrong. It had been a relief to go to bed early.

"This is her last night in our house." Letitia had said, and burst into noisy sobs. Samuel had gone to comfort her, tears glistening in his own eyes, and Marina had made her escape.

Downstairs had gone quiet now. Marina was in her night-things but hadn't even bothered to try and sleep. She knew that sleep wouldn't come. Worries and doubts kept assailing her. What if there'd been some other way, something she'd overlooked? What if the Duke played false, and didn't cancel the debt after all? He said that he couldn't put his father-in-law in gaol, but you could never tell with men like that.

Worries thronged around Marina, making her head throb. She felt sick and frightened, like a trapped animal whose last way of escape had just been cut off. She drew her knees up to her chest and wrapped her arms around them, curling up into a little ball in the centre of her bed.

What I wouldn't give to wake up and find that all this was a dream.

A knock came on Marina's door, making her jump and jerking her out of her spiralling thoughts.

She glanced up, seeing the flickering, yellow light of a candle coming from underneath her door. Was it Samuel, come to tell her that he couldn't allow this after all, or Letitia, here to give last minute advice and beg her to change her mind?

"It's me," Josephine answered. "Can I come in?"

Marina sniffled, rubbing at her eyes. She hoped she hadn't looked as if she were crying.

"Of course. The door isn't locked."

Josephine opened the door and slid inside. She was wearing a long, white nightgown that made her look even younger than her years, and was pale in the unsteady candlelight. She hurried over to Marina's bed, bare feet slapping on the cold floor, and climbed onto the bed beside her, placing the candlestick on the nightstand.

"It's really happening." Josephine said, after a pause. "You're really marrying him."

Marina shrugged. "That was always going to happen. What did you think would happen instead?"

Josephine bit her lip. "I don't know. I thought something would come up."

"So did I." Marina admitted. "But it didn't, so that's that. Besides, I'd rather marry the Duke than Lord Ellersby."

Josephine pulled a face. "Yes, he's awful. Does he know that you're marrying the Duke of Brixham instead of him? Has he said anything?"

Marina swallowed hard, remembering a hastily penned letter, full of insults and bile, directed to her in Lord Ellersby's handwriting. She'd thrown it in the fire and thanked her lucky stars that she'd escaped marrying that man.

"Yes, he knows. I don't want to talk about Lord Ellersby, though. I'm marrying the Duke. I'll be a duchess."

The title didn't seem to impress Josephine. She regarded Marina steadily, her eyes dark and intense in the inconstant candlelight.

"You're afraid." Josephine whispered.

A lump formed in Marina's throat. "Yes, I'm afraid. Of course I'm afraid. I'm marrying a strange man. I had considered the possibility of marrying a man I didn't love, but I never thought... oh, it doesn't matter. I think he's a good man, Josephine. I think I'll be happy with him."

"What if he's not? What if you aren't."

"Then I shall manage." Marina said steadily, pleased at her own composure. She needed to be strong for her family, and especially for Josephine. Josephine was far too young for all of this. Too young to have her future snatched away. Too young to see her sister and mother destitute, and her father consigned to Marshalsea. Really, Marina had made her decision for her sister just as much as for her father.

She slipped an arm around Josephine, pulling her close.

"I love you, Josephine." Marina said softly. "And I want you to grab life with both hands, you hear? I want you to be happy."

"I want you to be happy. You're sitting awake at this time of night, so I know that you're not happy right now."

Marina shrugged. "Tomorrow will come and go. I'll turn into a married woman from a single one, but the world will keep turning. You'll see."

Josephine didn't look convinced.

"Oh," she said, pulling back and fumbling in her pocket. "I almost forgot why I came."

She took out a pack of cards, and Marina broke into a grin.

They were old cards, gifted to Josephine by Samuel years ago. She'd learned to play poker with those cards, just like Marina.

"I thought we could while away the night with a few games." Josephine said, grinning and expertly shuffling the cards. "Maybe I'll beat you this time."

Marina chuckled. "I think not."

For the next hour, the only sound in the silent room was the shuffle and slide of cards, and the soft intakes of breath as good or bad hands were discovered. Mostly from Josephine, of course, since Marina was far too experienced to display any shock or surprise at whatever her cards had to offer.

It would be nice for this moment to last forever, Marina thought idly. Just me and Josie, playing cards on my bed. If only the sun would never come up.

That was a silly hope, of course. Midnight had already come and gone. The next day was here, and in a few short hours, morning and Marina's wedding would arrive. There was no escaping it, not really.

"You're brave, you know." Josephine said, breaking the silence first. Marina glanced up sharply, but her sister's eyes were on her cards. "Marrying him, I mean."

Marina swallowed. "I'm not sure I could call it brave. It's not as though there's anything else we can do."

Josephine shrugged. "It's Papa's mess. You could just let him work his way out of it."

"That's not kind."

"I'm not trying to be unkind. I'm just being honest. You're meant for something better than this, Marina."

Marina kept her eyes on her own cards, swallowing down the sharp lump in her throat. She didn't want Josephine to do this right now. She didn't want to be reminded that she could, even at this eleventh hour, get out of the marriage. Her parents would certainly not force her into it, even if it meant that the bailiffs would be here at dawn.

That, of course, was exactly why Marina had to go through with it.

"It's honour, Josephine." She said quietly. "I love Mama and Papa. I know Papa made mistakes – we all know that – but there's nothing we can do about it now. There's nothing he can do. Don't you think Papa's guilt is eating him up alive about all this? I see it in his face. He's so miserable,
because he thinks that he's ruined my life."

"He has." Josephine retorted, venom in her voice. "How could he do this, Marina? How can you forgive him so easily? It's not fair, you having to martyr yourself like this."

"I know it's not fair. We all know it. You, me, Mama, Papa. But life isn't fair. I don't mean that in an awful way, I just mean that sometimes awful things happen, and we find ourselves with no way out of it. Of course, if Papa had been more sensible with his money, this wouldn't have happened. He'll remember that for the rest of his life, you know."

"So he should." Josephine muttered.

"Don't be angry with him when I'm gone, please. If he does it again, then we can be angry at him. But right now, me marrying the Duke of Brixham is what our family needs, do you understand?"

Josephine pressed her lips together in a thin line.

"You're braver than me, Marina." She murmured; eyes still fixed on her cards. For a long time, neither of them moved, either to speak again or to lay down any cards.

Marina moved first, setting down a set of cards. She had a winning hand, but the victory tasted bitter.

They finished their game, and reluctantly set down the cards.

"Another round?" Josephine said, almost pleadingly.

Marina shook her head reluctantly. "We really ought to sleep, don't you think?"

Tears welled up in Josephine's eyes. "I can't believe that this is happening. I keep expecting it all to be a dream. A bad dream, the sort you're happy to wake up from."

Marina smiled weakly. "Me too. But still, I'm going to be a duchess. That's something, isn't it?"

"I suppose so." Josephine said, unwilling to concede the point. "You could run away, you know. I'd help you."

Marina reached out, patting Josephine's cheek. She felt, strangely enough, that if she were left alone everything would start to fall apart.

"I know you would, Josie. I know it."

Josephine got up hastily, turning her face away as if she didn't want her sister to see her cry. She lifted an arm, dashing the back of her hand across her eyes, and shoved the cards haphazardly into her pocket.

"I hope the Duke of Brixham plays cards with you, Marina." Josephine said, her voice choked.

"I'm sure he will, Josie. I'm sure he will."

Josephine snatched up her candle and hurried to the door. The hallway outside was dark and silent, letting in a gust of cold air that made Marina shiver, and made Josephine's candle flame gutter.

"Wait." Marina said impulsively, and Josephine stopped dead.

"What is it?"

"I need you to promise me something, Josephine."

"Anything."

Marina smiled wryly. "You don't even know what it is yet."

"It doesn't matter."

"Very well. I want you to promise me that when you come to marry…"

"I will never marry." Josephine interrupted.

"… well then, if you marry, I want you to marry for love. Do you understand, Josephine? Don't marry to oblige Mama and Papa, or because you feel like you ought to get married, or because you just want children, or you are afraid of being lonely. Marry for love, my sweet girl. There are other considerations, of course, but make sure you love the man."

A fat tear rolled down Josephine's round cheek, and this time she made no attempt to wipe it away.

"I will." she choked out, then fled into the hallway, letting the door close behind her.

Marina wept for a few minutes. She cried for the loss of her own future – not that she'd known what her own future held – and allowed herself to feel relieved that Josephine wouldn't be in the same situation as her. Josephine, at least, would have the freedom to choose.

A flash of red on the floor caught her eye, and Marina leaned forward to inspect it. It was a card, dropped from Josephine's pack of cards. It was the Queen of Hearts, which seemed remarkably apt. Marina picked it up, intending to return it later. In the morning, if she remembered.

Despite everything, she fell asleep, the card resting on the pillow beside her.

Chapter Ten

I really should go to bed, Adam thought, helping himself to another glass of brandy. He'd long since stopped looking at the clock. What would be the point in going to bed, really?

He'd only lie awake in bed, thinking about the time ticking by, moving towards morning and his wedding.

His wedding. He was getting married in the morning. What a strange idea. Adam sipped his brandy, feeling the warmth of the drink course through his veins. He would have a headache in the morning if he drank much more, and that was hardly fair on his poor bride-to-be.

Although, for all he knew, she could be drinking herself silly, too.

That idea wasn't a pleasant one. He imagined Marina, with those shockingly vivid hazel eyes, miserably drinking glass after glass of brandy or wine or punch, or whatever, trying to build up her courage to go through with the wedding.

Are we just going to make each other miserable? Adam thought, and his stomach heaved.

A tap on the door made him jump. He glanced at the clock, and saw that it was approaching half past one in the morning. Where had the time gone, and who was up at this hour? He'd told the servants to go to bed.

"Adam?" came Evelyn's muffled voice. "It's me."

"Mother? What are you doing up?"

The door creaked open, and Evelyn peered into the room. They hadn't spoken much since Adam had told her the news. He knew that his mother didn't approve, and that was that. She was coming to the wedding, though, and that was something.

"I wanted to talk to you." Evelyn said, letting herself in and closing the door behind her. "I kept telling myself that it was none of my business, and that it's all decided, but I couldn't sleep, so here I am."

Adam swallowed, setting aside his glass of brandy. "Well, come on in, and let's talk."

Evelyn did just that, settling herself in the armchair opposite Adam's. For a moment, they sat together in silence, both staring into the dying embers of the fire.

"I worry about your happiness, Adam." Evelyn said, her voice quiet.

"Has this something to do with my wedding tomorrow?"

Evelyn shot him a look. "Of course it is, you silly boy. Tell me, why are you marrying this young woman? And be honest with me, please. I think I deserve a little honesty, don't you?"

Adam bit his lip. "Well, this is the only way I'll get back my money from Lord Chelwood. If he goes to Marshalsea, the whole thing will be written off as a bad debt. I'll get some money from the sale of the house, but..."

Adam trailed off. That wasn't exactly a lie. He had loaned Lord Chelwood a substantial amount, to say nothing of the interest, and he certainly wanted his money back.

Evelyn's face hardened. She stared into the fire, something flickering in her eyes that Adam couldn't place.

"Your father was like that." she murmured. "He always thought of nothing but his money and his business, and how to get every last penny of other people. He always intended to turn you into a replica of himself, and now I see that he's done an excellent job of it. He's taught you well."

Adam swallowed reflexively, flinching as if his mother had struck him.

"I... I'm not a bad man, Mother. I'll make Lady Marina happy."

But Evelyn wasn't listening. She was still staring into the fire, lost in a memory.

"Your father and I married for love, you know." she said suddenly.

Adam blinked, sucking in a breath. It was strange, but he'd always assumed that his parents' marriage was one of convenience. They'd always been cold to each other, if polite and courteous. They were not a couple who were in love, and they had been that way for as long as Adam could remember.

"Love?" Adam echoed.

Evelyn nodded. "Yes, love. Your father was a different man when he was young to the man you knew. He was bold, confident, clever, interesting – oh, I was drawn to him immediately. His father disapproved of our match. He was a cold, calculating man. He hated me, and never bothered to hide it. But, I was well-bred and came with a sizeable fortune, and your father was of age and his only heir. We were married, and it was the happiest day of my life. It was the first time he ever truly stood up to his father." She sighed. "And it was the last, too."

The hairs on the back of Adam's neck prickled. "What do you mean?"

"I mean that I made a grave miscalculation. I ploughed through our troublesome engagement and dealt with his father – your grandfather – because I believed that everything would be different once we were married. I couldn't have been more wrong."

"What happened?"

Evelyn closed her eyes. "We moved into the family home. Your grandfather presided over the household. Your father had defied him in marrying me, and he was keen to make it up to him. I thought that your grandfather would want to make my life a misery, but in fact, he ignored me from that day on. I was no longer relevant, you see. Your father spent more and more time with your grandfather, and slowly but surely my influence was squeezed out. It took years, of course, but I soon saw what was happening. I tried to balance out your grandfather's influence, but I was so alone. The house – this house, in fact – was so different from what it is now. The servants despised me, encouraged by your grandfather, and the only friends we had were his friends, who naturally disliked me, too. The only true ally I had was your father, and I always had to fight tooth and nail for him against your grandfather." She shook her head, lifting a hand to wipe away a tear. "It was exhausting, and I could never get your father to understand what a cruel, ruthless man your grandfather was. He adored his papa, you see, as young men often do."

Adam swallowed down a lump in his throat. He imagined his mother, a younger version of her, drifting around the house, always alone. He'd never known his grandfather – he had only been a baby when the man died – but his picture hung in the Great Hall. He was an austere, unkind looking man, glowering down at whoever dared to pass underneath his picture.

He could imagine that man smirking triumphantly over the dinner table at his unfortunate daughter-in-law, revelling in her discomfort and his mother being helpless.

"Father really didn't know?" he said, his voice small.

Evelyn shook her head. "If he did know, he kept it quiet. I think he saw what he wanted to see. When his father finally died – and I am not proud of this – I was thrilled. At last, I thought that we could be a real family. Your father was spending hardly any time with me and you, because your grandfather told him that a 'real man' shouldn't dawdle around in a nursery and ladies' parlours. It wasn't manly to love one's wife, it seemed."

"Oh, Mother. I'm so sorry."

"Perhaps it was a punishment for being so happy over the man's death, but your father changed after that. He didn't try with me anymore. He mourned his father, and I could see that he carried a heavy weight of guilt. He regretted not being the man his father wanted, and clearly intended to make up for it now. He never did start spending time with me again. I think his love was already waning, but your grandfather's death killed it off altogether. He became absorbed in his business, focused on earning money and establishing a reputation as a heartless man of business. And later, of course, in training you to be the same sort of person."

There was a pause while Adam absorbed this. This story did not match the glowing, admiring tales his father had told him about his grandfather, but he never doubted for a moment that they were true. His mother did not lie, and her words had the ring of truth in any case.

"I never knew." He murmured.

Evelyn smiled wryly. "Sometimes, I want to take my father-in-law's picture down from the Great Hall and smash it into a thousand pieces."

Adam had to smile at that. "I can see why. I'm sorry, Mother. I never knew that you felt like that."

Evelyn's smile faded off her face.

"Regret heavily marked all of our lives. Your grandfather regretted marrying a woman for her money – she was long dead before I met your father, probably dead of neglect and misery – and your father regretted marrying me for love, and going against his father. And you – oh, Adam, my darling boy, I'm so afraid that you'll regret marrying this woman to settle her father's debts."

"I can't go back on my word now, Mother." Adam said quietly. "You wanted me to marry, didn't you? I just want you to be happy."

"Well, I want you to be happy. I want you to live life free of regret, secure in the knowledge you make the right choice."

"Do you think that breaking things off with Marina Cornish would be the right thing to do, and sending her father to Marshalsea?"

Evelyn turned away. "That's a cruel thing to say, Adam. Sometimes I think there's nothing left of the little boy I raised. How can you be so heartless? How can you force a young woman into marriage because of the sins of others?"

"She chose this."

"That is not an excuse, and you know it. What choice did she have, truly?"

Adam flushed, turning away. "It's too late now, Mother. The wedding is going ahead. I'm sorry that you don't agree, but it's not as if I'll make her unhappy. I'll be a good husband, I promise. Besides, you'll be here."

Evelyn eyed him for a long moment, disappointment visible in every line of her face. Adam felt the childish urge to burst into tears and throw himself into his mother's arms, begging forgiveness and promising to do the right thing from now on.

But he was a man, and too large to fling himself into Evelyn's arms. Adam stayed where he was, long fingers wrapped around the brandy glass.

"Very well. Evelyn said finally. "You've made your decision, that much is clear. I suppose I shall see you in the morning, for the wedding."

She got up shakily, and began to move towards the door. She paused, hand on the door handle, as if she wanted to say something. Adam held his breath, waiting.

But Evelyn only gave her head a light shake and disappeared into the hallway.

Adam was left alone. The silence was unbearable where it had been peaceful before. The ticking of the clock was obscenely loud, reminding Adam that some decisions could no more be reversed than the hands of the clock could go back in time. He lifted his glass of brandy to his lips, but the smell turned his stomach now. He'd had enough – more than enough.

He set the glass aside and sank down in his seat. Adam still wasn't tired, but was balefully aware of the time ticking by, faster and faster. Would he appear, bleary and red-eyed, at his own wedding tomorrow? Of course, it wasn't as if there would be many people there.

Adam raised his eyes to the large portrait of his father, sitting above the fireplace. When he was young, a portrait of his grandfather had sat there. Now, it made Adam feel sick and disappointed.

"What would you make of all this, I wonder?" Adam said aloud, addressing the picture. "And should I even listen to your advice? What have you made me, Father? All I ever wanted was to be like you, and all Mother wanted was that I should be nothing like you at all. Or Grandfather, for that matter. Somehow, I've managed to disappoint you both. That's a trick, isn't it?"

He rubbed a hand over his face, feeling the exhaustion of the day settle onto his shoulders. There was no use thinking about tomorrow. Adam knew he would not cancel the wedding. He was going to be married to Lady Marina Cornish, and that was that. It was too late to change his mind, and Adam wasn't even sure whether he wanted to.

Of course, that might be the brandy, muddying his senses and slowing his thinking. Had his mother ever even met Lady Marina, or her parents? He thought not and felt a pang of guilt. He ought to have introduced them.

The clock began to chime two o' clock in the morning, the sonorous sounds counting out the hours. Five hours before he would have to start getting ready for his wedding. Seven hours before he would become a married man, and Lord Chelwood's debt was written off and forgotten forever.

Adam rested his head against the back of the seat and closed his eyes. He knew he wouldn't bother going upstairs tonight. He'd sleep here, like he used to when there was too much work to be done.

Had his father done the same, when he was younger? What would Marina Cornish think of his habits? Would she be as miserable as his mother had been in her marriage?

No point thinking of that now, Adam thought, resigned. It's

happening. Better hope I'm making the right choice.

Chapter Eleven

"Wake up, your ladyship. It's time to get up."

Marina jerked awake, pulled abruptly out of confusing and frightening dreams into reality, which was every bit as bewildering.

It was Louisa who had woken her, the kindly head housemaid, who often doubled as ladies' maid these days.

Ladies' maids were too expensive.

Louisa placed a hearty breakfast tray down beside her, and the smell of fried bacon and roasted sausages drifted to Marina's nose. Her stomach convulsed, and she turned her face into the pillow.

"I don't want that, Louisa. I'm sorry, I'm just not hungry."

Louisa pressed her lips together. "You need some nourishment, your ladyship. It's your wedding day."

That didn't make the nausea any better.

"Come on, let's have a look at you." Louisa said, obviously trying to sound cheerful and encouraging.

Reluctantly, Marina sat up. Louisa winced.

"Oh, your ladyship, you didn't sleep well, did you? You look a little... tired."

"Thank you, Louisa, that's very encouraging." Marina huffed, flinging back the sheets. She padded over to her dresser mirror, and reluctantly glanced at her own face inside.

Louisa had not been exaggerating.

Marina had slept badly, and it was written on her face. Her eyes were bloodshot and puffy, ringed with black shadows, and she was horribly pale. Her hair stuck up, and although that would brush out, it was lanky and greasy, in great need of a wash.

Marina guilty remembered how careless she'd been over her appearance lately. There'd been no need to dress up and look nice, after all. The family didn't go anywhere – they couldn't afford to do so – and there would no chance of Marina ever attracting a gentleman to fall in love with her. She was marrying Lord Brixham, and that was that.

The only problem was that she was marrying him today.

"I look a sight." Marina moaned.

"Not to worry, your ladyship." Louisa informed her briskly.

"We've got time. I'll run you a nice bath. Eat your breakfast while you're waiting.

Marina sat numbly on her bed, picking at cold toast, congealed eggs, and once-crispy bacon that had run to fat and salt. The servants hurried past her with buckets of hot water, gradually filling up the huge copper tub in Marina's washroom.

She always felt guilty over how much work went into her baths. Still, all of the servants flashed her an encouraging smile. Of course, they all knew about the marriage, and the circumstances of said marriage.

They pity me, Marina thought. I pity myself.

Louisa eyed Marina, chewing her lip.

"You don't look yourself, your ladyship."

Marina shrugged. "I don't feel myself, Louisa."

Louisa shuffled over, sitting beside her on the edge of the bed. It was a shocking breach of protocol for a maid – or any servant, really – to sit in the presence of their lord or lady. Louisa was taking a chance doing such a thing.

Marina could have hugged her. It felt, just for a moment, as if they were equals. Two young women, with their lives ahead of them, curious as to what the future might hold.

Louisa reached out, taking Marina's hand in hers.

"It's a fine thing, what you're doing for your family." She murmured. "We're proud of you. All of us. I know... well, that's not right, is it. I don't know anything about this. But I imagine that it's not easy. But you keep your chin up and know what a wonderful thing you're doing."

Marina smiled weakly at her. "Thank you, Louisa. I've been dreading this day, but now that it's here, I can just get it over with, can't I?"

"That's the spirit, your ladyship. Just get through today, and then the rest of your life can begin. You'll be rewarded for this, I'm sure of it."

"I wish I was sure of it."

Louisa bit her lip and said nothing to that. After a moment, she got to her feet again, shaking out her skirts and apron.

"Come along, your ladyship. Your bath is ready."

***

Marina leaned back against the side of the tub, the sheet draped against the sides feeling hot and soft against her skin. The water was deliciously warm, scented with lavender and rose petals, baby soft and fragrant.

It was impressive how a simple bath could make a person feel better. Alone in her washroom, Marina could almost forget that in a few hours she'd be marrying a stranger, a man that she barely knew, let alone liked, and that her life would be different from this day on.

Somehow, those problems felt far away right now. At the moment, Marina was relaxed, warm, and happy. Her skin felt clean and well-scrubbed, her hair smelt good, and the water lapping around her shoulders hadn't lost its core of warmth.

I could stay here forever, Marina thought, resting her head against the sheets and closing her eyes.

On cue, the washroom door opened.

Louisa and Letitia appeared, and Marina gave a sigh. There went her peaceful soak.

"You are looking much better, your ladyship." Louisa said approvingly, glancing at Letitia for approval.

Letitia didn't seem to have slept well, either. She had dark rings around her eyes and seemed a little older than her years today. However, she had a bright, determinedly cheerful smile pinned to her face.

It wasn't reassuring. Quite the opposite, in fact.

"Yes, you look very fresh, darling." Letitia said, flashing an encouraging smile at her daughter. "Now, get out of the bath and get dried off. I have something to show you."

"What is it?" Marina asked, feeling around for the soft towel.

Usually, a lady – especially a lady of Marina's status – would have a handful of servants to attend her while she bathed. Once again, this was a luxury they could no longer afford. The servants were far too busy to wait on their employers while they bathed.

Frankly, Marina preferred her privacy when she bathed. However, if the truth came out that the Cornish family could not afford sufficient staff for such "basic" necessities as bathing assistance, they would be a laughing stock.

Although there was a good chance that they were already a laughingstock.

Louisa stepped into the washroom to help Marina towel off, while Letitia scurried back into the bedroom.

"What's the surprise?" Marina asked.

Louisa chuckled. "Well, if I told you, it wouldn't be a surprise, would it? I'm not about to ruin the nicest thing about your wedding for you."

Marina stepped out of the washroom with Louisa in tow, still warm and steaming from her bath.

The first thing she saw was the dress.

It was a beautiful gown, and no mistake. The design was clearly a wedding dress. It was all white satin, the skirt puffed out by ruffles and crinoline petticoats, with expensive lace hemming the waist, neckline, and capped sleeves. It was not a simple design, as was the fashion right now, but something elaborate and exquisite. It was clear that hundreds of hours of work had gone into the dress, not to mention the finest, prettiest fabrics available.

Pearls and sequins studded the bodice, glittering and sparkling in the light. The pearls and sequins trailed down the front of skirts in the shape of a V, enhancing the shine and making the wearer almost seem to have scales. A simple lace veil hung over the shoulders, ending a few inches above the hem.

It was a beautiful, beautiful dress, and a familiar one.

"This is your wedding gown, Mama." Marina managed, a lump in her throat threatening to choke her. "I... I can't wear your wedding gown."

"Why? Don't you want to?" Letitia asked anxiously. "Oh, darling, have I made a mistake?"

Marina wanted to laugh and cry at the same time. "No, of course not! Mama, you know how I adore that dress. It's the most beautiful thing I've seen. I've always said..." she couldn't quite finish the sentence.

Fortunately – or unfortunately – Letitia finished it for her.

"You always wanted to wear it for your wedding day." Letitia murmured softly. "Well, here it is."

Marina shook her head. "It doesn't feel right, Mama. This... this doesn't feel like a proper wedding. I know it's silly, but that's how I feel."

Letitia shot a tiny glance at Louisa, who immediately took her cue and slipped out of the room. Left alone, mother and daughter turned to each other, wrapping their arms around each other.

"This is your wedding day, my darling girl." Letitia murmured. "I know it doesn't feel like this, but a wedding day only comes once. This is it, Marina. I know... I know it's not what you dreamt of. It's certainly not what we dreamt of for you. But you've always been such a clever, practical girl, and I know you won't dwell on what might have been."

"I won't. It's a waste of time." Marina hiccoughed.

Letitia planted a kiss on the top of Marina's head. "It's always been your dream to wear this dress, just as it's been my dream to see you wear it. I had hoped... hoped that the circumstances would be different, but they are not. But at least you'll wear it, and I'll see you wear it. This dress brought me luck, you know. I married your papa in it, and while he's not perfect, he is without a doubt the love of my life. Perhaps you'll meet the love of your life in this gown, too."

Marina snorted. "You can't be talking about the Duke of Brixham. He doesn't love me."

Letitia swallowed hard. "I know, darling. But love can develop in marriage. I know that might seem like the sort of thing parents tell their children when they want to marry the people they've picked out for them, but it's true. Growing up, I had friends who married for convenience or to oblige their parents, and fell deeply in love afterwards."

Marina pulled away, wiping her eyes with the back of her hand.

"And I'm sure you knew people who hated each other before and after their marriage, too."

She immediately regretted speaking. Her mother's face twisted in anguish.

"My darling girl, do you hate the duke? It's not too late to call all this off."

Marina closed her eyes. "I don't hate him, Mama. I don't

know him. Hate is a strong word. I suppose I am... indifferent towards him."

That was a lie, and Marina knew it as soon as it left her lips. It was true, she did not know the Duke, and what she did know about him was not favourable. But there'd been something between the two of them, something compelling and tangible. She wasn't entirely sure whether it was good or bad, but one thing was abundantly clear.

It was not indifference.

Letitia sighed. "Well, indifference can turn to something good, can't it, my dearest? I'm sure that when the Duke sees you in this gown, he'll fall in love with you right there and then."

Marina had to smile at that. "You never know, Mama."

Encouraged, Letitia pressed on. "I know he seems very severe and unfriendly, but I'm sure that's just a façade. Men feel as if they have to behave like that, you know. His father was an unpleasant man, if I remember correctly, and that does have an influence on a young man. I've heard the rumours about the Duke, and I'm afraid that some of them are true. But even if he does have a heart of ice, you are without a doubt the woman to melt it. I don't know how he could be around you and not fall in love with you."

Marina smiled weakly, not wanting to contradict her mother. It was clear that Letitia believed every word she said and did not understand how anyone might not love her darling girl.

She'd missed a crucial point, though. Marina was not the beautiful, delightful nymph that Letitia clearly thought that she was, and the Duke did not have a heart of ice.

No, not ice. Nothing so fragile. The Duke was a man of marble, exquisitely carved but entirely cold and lifeless. You couldn't melt marble, could you?

But that was neither helpful nor necessary to say. Marina kept a cheerful smile pinned on her face while the dressing process began. She smoothed her palms down the silky, heavy fabric of The Gown – which she'd always called her mother's wedding dress in her head – unable to believe that she was wearing it.

It felt wrong. It felt as though she were wearing the wedding dress to the wrong event, like a garden party or to promenade in the Park.

This is my wedding day. This can't be happening, Marina thought numbly. I can't be getting married today.

She knew, of course, that she only had to speak and the wedding would be called off. That made it much harder to stay strong.

We need this. Papa will go to gaol if I don't marry this man. Mama and Josephine will be ruined. This must happen. There's no other way.

No other way.

The words clanged round and round in her head, deafening and drowning out everything else.

"If you're ready, darling," Letitia said softly, "It's time to go."

Chapter Twelve

An awkward silence had developed between Adam and Evelyn on the way to the chapel. It was to be expected, really.

Perhaps she thought he'd change his mind. He'd certainly hoped that she would change theirs.

Part of Adam had been anxious that his mother would refuse to attend the wedding at all. That would be shameful, and something he'd always regret. He wanted his mother there.

And here she was, so that was a relief.

Evelyn had chosen a deep maroon gown, decorated with pearls and a fur trim. It wasn't really the proper dress for a wedding, but it suited her well, and Adam was simply glad that she was here.

In hindsight, he should have chosen an earlier hour for the ceremony. The London streets were already thronged with people, carriages, and carts, and there would certainly be a few people in the chapel, eager to get a good look at a real Lord and Lady getting married.

Adam didn't want an audience. He wanted to get the ceremony over as quickly and cleanly as possible, and he suspected that Lady Marina felt the same.

"If this traffic doesn't let up, we'll be late." Adam observed, more to break the silence than anything.

That was another sign of weakness that the old Duke would have frowned upon. Never be the first to break a handshake, a stare, or the silence.

Evelyn sighed. "Perhaps it wouldn't be the worst thing if that happened."

Adam's jaw tightened. "Let's not talk about this now, Mother."

"Then when should we talk about it? Tomorrow, perhaps, when you're freshly married and it's too late to do anything about it?"

"Mother, please."

"I just hope you don't come to regret it, that's all. Unfortunately, I think you will regret it. Very much, and very soon."

Anger surged up inside Adam, mixed with frustration and a

niggling pang of fear.

"I don't think that's fair. You're the one who was so keen for me to marry, after all. And now I am getting married, you're sulking."

Evelyn tutted. "Don't talk to me like I'm a child, Adam. Really, you do remind me so much of your father at times."

Adam flinched at that, turning back towards the window. The silence returned, but only lasted a minute or so this time.

"I'm sorry." Evelyn said softly. "That was... uncalled for."

Adam shrugged. "My father was a great man. I should be honoured to be like him."

He knew that his mother was looking at him, her gaze burning into the side of his face. Adam resolutely didn't look.

"You shouldn't be."

He pretended he hadn't heard, leaning forward as if to survey the crowded streets.

"We're nearly there now. You will be pleasant to Lady Marina, won't you?"

Evelyn was engrossed in rearranging her skirts and twisting the pearl bracelet on her wrist.

"Of course I will. The poor girl is probably miserable and distraught."

Adam swallowed hard. "You know, some mothers might think highly of their sons, and claim that any lady would be lucky to marry them. Why can't you be one of those mothers?"

Evelyn didn't bat an eyelid. "I'm not in the habit of telling you pleasant lies, Adam. Your father's father only ever told him what he wanted to hear and look how he turned out. I will stand by you because you are my son and I love you, but I will also tell you the truth, no matter how hard it is to hear."

Adam sighed, leaning back against the seat. "Very well, Mother. I could ask for no more. But it is unfair that you're so against this marriage when you were the one who..."

"Are we to go over this again and again? I feel like I'm on a merry-go-round, and I can't get off. I wanted you to choose a wife carefully, somebody you could love. Of course, love isn't always practical, and so you might choose a wife based on friendship and mutual respect. That would be fine, too. I didn't intend for you to marry the daughter of one of your debtors in exchange for the debt being written off. Not only is that a deeply inauspicious start, but you are also beginning the marriage on unequal footing, and with terrible motives. Can you not see why this is a bad idea?"

Adam bit his lip. "I can, but I thought of this before I finalized the marriage. There's always a risk with marriage, is there not?"

"Not so much risk, Adam."

"Well, it's done now." he said briskly, turning to look out of the window. "Or almost done, at least."

"We can still call it off."

"Would that be honourable, Mother?"

Evelyn hesitated, caught between the stark truth and what she wanted to say.

"No." she admitted. "It would not. The lady can call off the wedding at this point, but not you, my son. I'm sorry."

He shrugged. "There it is, then. This is happening, so let's make the best of it."

Silence descended again. The carriage crawled on, making its way through the crowds. Adam entertained a brief fantasy in which they did not get there in time, and the irate Cornish family called off the whole thing, and would not be placated.

A silly fantasy, of course. Lord Chelwood needed this marriage much more than Adam did, and wouldn't call it off under any circumstances.

He dredged up a memory of Lady Marina, inspecting her in his mind's eye as a potential bride. She was pretty, that was certain, and had a spark and spirit about her that he admired. She'd stood up to him in defence of her father, which was doubly admirable, and struck him as an intelligent, capable sort of woman.

He could do worse for a bride. There were any number of vapid, empty-headed young women in Society, who were remarkably beautiful and incredibly rich, but boasted no other qualities beside that.

Except, of course, for the accomplishments necessary to flourish in Society. Adam thought he would rather have a wife who could balance an account book, or spend her days with her nose in a book, than one who could play a perfect but soulless minuet for the entertainment of others.

It struck him then that he had no idea what Lady Marina liked to do for hobbies. Perhaps she was a minuet lady, or one who lived to dance and drink and laugh.

Not that it mattered, of course. She could do more or less what she liked when they were married. If she wanted to fill her days with pianoforte playing, watercolours, and short, ladylike walks, that was her business.

The carriage jerked to a halt, waking Adam from his musings. He leaned forward, peering out of the window.

"We're here." He announced brusquely, trying to ignore the flurry of nerves in the pit of his stomach.

He looked around to find his mother staring at him, worry and pity mingling in her eyes.

"Don't look at me like that, Mother."

"Like what?"

"Like you feel sorry for me. Like I'm a silly child who won't listen to reason."

Evelyn sighed. "You are a silly child, Adam. I hate to be the first to inform you. As your mother, I will always see you as a child in any case. Now, come on, let's go inside. You and I have a wedding to get through."

Taking a deep breath as if she were about to plunge over a cliff, Evelyn scrambled past him and out of the carriage.

Adam followed her. There wasn't much else he could do, after all.

***

St Frederick's Chapel was a small, run-down place, with a small to moderately-sized congregation, and a roof much in need of repairing.

Adam very much regretted organizing the ceremony to take place here. He'd chosen the small, little-known place in the hopes of privacy, and of course that hadn't happened. The back two rows of the chapel were full of strangers. Busy-bodies, gossips, and bored youths interested to see ladies and gentlemen going about their business. The priest was a thin, timid man with a permanent sheen of sweat across his forehead, which he perpetually dabbed at with a stained handkerchief.

He couldn't seem to quite manage to look Adam in the eyes, and kept opening the Bible he held and muttering under his breath, as if rehearsing the words.

"How many weddings have you done?" Adam asked brusquely, making the poor man jump.

"W-Weddings, your Grace?" the man stammered. "Oh, many. Many. Too many to count, I'd say."

"Then there's no need to be quite so nervous."

He flushed. "I have never married a duke, your Grace."

Adam shrugged, already losing interest. "It's exactly like marrying an ordinary person. Same vows, same promise, same end result. It doesn't need to be a showy event. In fact, I'd appreciate a little brevity."

The priest nodded vigorously, dropping his head as if in shame, like he'd been scolded.

Did he feel like he'd been scolded? Adam bit his lip, and made a mental note not to take that tone with his future wife.

On cue, the doors opened. Adam flinched, turning around with something like anticipation in his chest.

He was disappointed.

Lord and Lady Chelwood hurried up the aisle, with their daughter, Lady Josephine, trailing along behind them.

Lord Chelwood avoided Adam's eye. Lady Chelwood looked as if she'd been crying and was on the brink of tears yet again. Lady Josephine was mulish and angry, glaring at Adam with obvious distaste.

Something twinged inside Adam that may or may not have been guilt. He ignored it, of course.

"Good day to you all." He said shortly, instead. "Where is Lady Marina?"

"She's outside." Lord Chelwood answered, mopping his

brow. "She's coming in soon. The maid is helping her prepare."

"Very good." Adam was perfectly prepared to wait in silence, but of course that wasn't about to happen.

Lady Josephine stepped forward; her arms crossed.

"You had better be nice to my sister and make her happy, or else."

"Josephine!" Lady Chelwood gasped, scandalised.

Behind him, Evelyn chuckled quietly to herself.

Adam raised an eyebrow, meeting Lady Josephine's furious stare.

"Your sister will become a duchess. She'll be able to do whatever she wants. I daresay she'll be happy enough."

This seemed to reassure Lord and Lady Chelwood, who cast quick, relieved glances at each other, but Lady Josephine was clearly not convinced. She narrowed her eyes.

"I'll be watching you very closely." She informed him, lifting her chin.

Evelyn cackled again, and Adam fought to suppress a smile.

"I should expect no less, Lady Josephine."

He made a bow, a low, flourishing affair that wouldn't have been out of place in a royal court. That sufficiently perplexed Lady Josephine enough for her mother to grab her and haul her away.

Then the doors at the back of the church opened, and everyone turned around.

Adam included.

His breath caught in his throat, which it had absolutely no right to do.

Lady Marina was wearing a wedding dress, which he hadn't expected. He'd supposed that she would wear one of her best dresses – he was wearing one of his finest suits, in an attractive shade of midnight blue – but this was a real wedding dress.

The gown dripped with satin, silk, lace, pearls, and sequins. It glittered when the light hit it, and although the shape and cut was distinctly old-fashioned, it suited Lady Marina to perfection. She wore it well, with her head held high and her glossy chestnut-coloured hair was piled on top of her head, curls cascaded cleverly down around her face and neck.

In short, she looked truly beautiful.

She looked like a bride.

If only she were smiling.

There was no shy, excited smile on Lady Marina's face. Her expression was set and grim, like she was walking to an execution rather than to the altar. The on-lookers exclaimed at her dress, whispering excitedly among themselves.

Fools, Adam thought, with a rush of venom. You don't know what's
happening here.

Lady Chelwood gave a teary sniffle into her handkerchief. Tears were not out of place at a wedding, but they were meant to be tears of joy, not sadness.

Once again, that irritating pang of conscience returned, and once again, Adam smothered it. There was no point in feeling guilt, or regret, or anything like that. Besides, it was too late to call anything off now.

Lady Marina reached the altar and flashed a tight-lipped smile all round.

"You look very beautiful, Lady Marina." Adam said. He'd planned to say something encouraging, but now the words seemed to fall flat.

"Thank you, your Grace." Lady Marina replied calmly. "As do you."

He fought the urge to smile. Far from being reassured, she seemed annoyed at his weak compliment.

That was good. Adam was aware that he tended to get what he wanted far too easily. Money, influence, and good looks could do that for a person, although it thoroughly destroyed their character in the process.

He and Lady Marina turned, side by side, to face the nervous priest.

The priest glanced between them, as if asking a question.

"I... may I begin?"

Adam opened his mouth to say something sharp, but remembered that Lady Marina was standing beside him, and closed it again. The man's timidity was annoying, but then Adam knew that he could be rather imposing.

"Of course." Adam said mildly. "Whenever you are ready."

"Excellent." The priest said, looking a little encouraged. "Dearly beloved, we are gathered here today..."

Chapter Thirteen

Adam handed his new bride into the carriage ahead of him, then Evelyn. He climbed in last of all, and the footmen closed the door behind them.

Lord and Lady Chelwood stood in front of the chapel, ashen faced, waving goodbye to their daughter. They looked heartbroken. Lady Josephine stood beside them, looking grim.

Marina took a seat on one side of the carriage, and Evelyn sat on the opposite side. After a moment's consideration, Adam sat beside his mother. Then the carriage gave a lurch forward and they were off, leaving the chapel, the nervy priest, and Marina's family behind.

Silence descended, thick and uncomfortable. Adam was vaguely aware of Marina shooting quick, nervous glances in his direction, which he studiously avoided.

He was married. He had just got married to the daughter of one of his debtors – no, not his debtor anymore, he had to remember that – and the reality of the situation sent Adam's mind reeling.

He was a married man. Married to the admittedly beautiful young woman sitting opposite.

The silence advanced from uncomfortable to downright unbearable. Marina kept her gaze fixed down at her lap now, twisting her fingers together, not speaking. Adam frantically tried to think of something, anything to say. He had the strangest feeling that if they reached his ducal home without speaking to each other, things would only go from bad to worse.

After all, if they couldn't speak to each other in the confines of a carriage, why on earth would they bother speaking to each other in Adam's vast family home?

Evelyn saved the day, as usual.

She leaned forward, reaching out to place a hand on Marina's knee. Marina flinched, but didn't jerk her leg away.

"I've prepared a delicious luncheon for us all when we return home, Marina. I wasn't sure what dishes you preferred, so I had

Cook make a selection. Do you like lamb? Salmon? Oh, and one of Cook's specialities is roasted cauliflower with cheese. Do you think you'd enjoy that?"

Marina gave a weak smile. "That sounds delicious, your Grace, thank you."

Evelyn beamed. "Goodness, child, there's no need to stand on ceremony with us anymore! Your Grace, indeed! My name is Evelyn, and I'm very pleased to meet you. I'm sure we'll get along famously."

Marina's smile got a little stronger, and she seemed to settle more comfortably into her seat. For some reason, that made Adam want to smile himself. He was aware, in a disinterested sort of way, that he wanted his new bride to be comfortable and at home around him and his mother, but had no idea how to set about doing that.

The old Duke had been very concise and firm about how to make people feel uncomfortable and guilty, but hadn't really touched on how to set them at their ease.

"I know there's been no wedding breakfast organized." Evelyn went on. "Now, I felt like we should have set up one regardless – is this not a wedding, after all? – but Adam was very firm. No celebrations, he said. But don't worry, the luncheon I've prepared will feel like a wedding breakfast, just for the three of us."

"You shouldn't have gone to so much trouble, Mother." Adam said sharply, before he even knew what he was doing. "I said no fuss, didn't I? Why did you go behind my back? There was no need to set up such an elaborate luncheon."

As soon the words were out of his mouth, Adam could have bitten off his tongue. Hurt flashed across Evelyn's face, and she bit her lip, turning away.

He cursed himself and his thoughtless words. What was he thinking, speaking so sharply to his mother? He was already more impertinent and short than most gentlemen would be to their mothers, and Evelyn had the patience of a saint.

And yet, here he was, berating her without cause, in front of his new wife, no less. Evelyn had turned scarlet and didn't say anything further. While Adam was groping for something to say that would undo all the damage he'd done, Marina spoke up.

"The luncheon sounds thrilling, your Gr – Evelyn." Marina said, leaning forward with a smile. "I'm absolutely starving. I missed breakfast, you see."

That did the trick. Evelyn's face lit up, and she cast a quick, triumphant glance at Adam.

"Oh, you poor dear! If only you'd said, we could have arranged something to eat before the ceremony."

"I think I was far too nervous to eat." Marina said, with a nervous laugh. "But I can't wait to tuck into the luncheon you've arranged."

She glanced at Adam, as if daring him to speak harshly again to his mother.

Start as you mean to go on, he reproved himself. Do you want the girl to think you're an absolute brute?

"You're quite right, Lady Marina." He said aloud. "Of course you must be hungry. My apologies, Mother. I was only thinking of myself, I'm afraid. I am rarely very hungry in the morning."

He cast a quick, apologetic glance at his mother, and hoped that it would be accepted. She narrowed her eyes briefly, then sighed, shaking her head.

"Yes, Adam can be a little thoughtless at times. None of us are perfect, though, are we? Now, Marina – may I call you Marina?"

"Of course, your Grace. Evelyn, I mean. I would like that very much."

"Wonderful. Well, Marina, I must tell you that we have a remarkable cook at our home. You'll love her concoctions. She's a genius, plain and simple. Of course, you will now be the lady of the house, and I daresay you'll want to make changes..."

"Actually, I..." Marina paused, glancing nervously at Adam again. "I don't know how to run a ducal house. I'm a fast learner, but I have no desire to go barging in and changing everything. I'd be grateful for whatever advice you can give me, Evelyn."

That was possibly the best thing she could have said. Evelyn's face lit up.

"Well, you are in luck, my dear. After the luncheon – and once you've settled in, of course – I'll give you the Grand Tour. The house is a beautiful one, full of history. There's lots to see, of course, and I daresay you'll find it remarkable. It's your house now, after all."

Adam watched bewilderment and panic cross Marina's face. It was clear that while she knew the purpose of her marriage, she hadn't given much thought to the logistics of it all.

As in, the fact that she was now a duchess, with a duchess' responsibilities.

And the world would be watching.

"It's quite... quite a lot to take in, isn't it?" she gasped, forcing a smile. She met Adam's eye across the carriage, and this time she held his gaze.

Adam was vaguely aware of a prickling heat spreading across his chest, not unlike the flutters of anxiety he'd felt as a child, before his father had firmly dealt with any such feelings.

He turned to glance out of the window, breaking their gaze and banishing those uncomfortable thoughts. He left Evelyn to rattle on to her new daughter-in-law, clearly thrilled at the idea of having another woman about the place.

He was glad that Marina seemed to be a kind sort of woman, who wouldn't belittle Evelyn and try and push her out of the house. He just wished he could maintain a more neutral feeling around her. There was something about Marina that got under his skin, and Adam wasn't sure he disliked the feeling.

Chapter Fourteen

How much longer was it going to be?

Marina fought to sit still, resisting the urge to fidget and wriggle in her seat. On long carriage journeys with her family, they would play card games, or chat, or just read their books, content in each other's company.

This was something else.

The Dowager Duchess – or Evelyn, as she'd insisted on being called – was chattering away, clearly eager to have another female to talk with. She seemed like a pleasant, friendly sort of woman, not at all like the icy, disapproving harridan of Marina's imagination.

She let the chatter wash over her, smiling and nodding at the right places. All the while, the Duke's presence seemed to burn into her awareness like a flame. He was just there, sitting across the carriage from her – he'd chosen not to sit beside her, she'd noticed – saying nothing.

Didn't he get bored? He had no book, no card games, nothing to occupy himself with except for conversation, and he wasn't even partaking in that.

At the moment, the Duke was staring out of the window, watching the scenery flash. His expression was impassive, despite the beauty around them. It was as if he were barely watching it.

"We're almost there now." Evelyn said, cutting into Marina's thoughts. "Just a little further, my dear. All of these lands belong to Adam, you see. Oh, look, some of the tenants have come out! Wave to them, dear."

Marina leaned forward, ready to oblige.

She'd expected to see waif-like peasants, grubby and tired and miserable, waving with dead eyes at a nobleman's carriage.

The reality was a little more unexpected.

They were passing through a small village, with well-maintained houses and well-thatched roofs, and a small cluster of people had come out to wave. They all looked healthy and well-fed, and a group of children – healthy, happy, and mischievous-looking – began to run alongside the carriage.

"God bless you, missis!" one of the children yelled.

"That's your Grace to you, Ted Burkins!" shouted a woman from the crowd, ostensibly his mother.

An elderly lady stood on the side of the road, with a basket full of flowers. She summoned over one of the children and handed her a little posy of flowers. The child eagerly raced along beside the carriage, holding up the posy.

"For you, miss – I mean, your Grace." The little girl panted.

Marina reached out of the carriage and took the posy.

"Thank you." she said, smiling, and met the old woman's eye. "Thank you, madam! These are beautiful."

The old woman raised a gnarled hand in acknowledgement.

"You have married a fine man, your Grace." She called. "My blessings."

Marina blinked at that, but before she could respond, the carriage turned a corner, leaving the village behind.

She sat back in her seat, inspecting the flowers. They were wildflowers, vividly coloured and smelling beautiful, tied at the stems with a length of twine.

"That's Corbridge Tow." Evelyn explained. "The village, I mean. It's the nearest one to our house. I must take you along to meet them all in person some time, they're fabulously hospitable. Wonderful tenants."

"They think that you're a wonderful man." Marina said, glancing at Adam. "Don't they know that you're a debt collector? A moneylender?"

Adam looked at her properly for the first time that day and flashed a sharp-toothed grin.

"Indeed, madam, but I don't exactly collect money from them, do I? Aside from the rent, of course, which is reasonably priced and eminently affordable, and pays to keep their houses in good condition and their wages well paid."

Marina said nothing. She wouldn't give him the satisfaction of knowing that she was surprised. No doubt he knew her opinion of him and was waiting for her to seem surprised or even dubious.

"We're almost here." Evelyn said. "Take a look out of the window, my dear, and you'll see your first glimpse of Blackburn Manor."

Marina leaned forward and peered out.

She saw the great house immediately, perched high on a craggy hill. There was something Gothic about it, with its almost cathedral-like design, large windows, and curved masonry.

It was beautiful, for certain, but also somewhat forbidding. The carriage began to travel uphill at a sharp angle, the wind picking up and the sky darkening. This high up in the countryside, it would be colder than down in the valley, and Marina shivered.

As they approached, she spotted a line of people standing outside the huge, iron-studded oak doorway, and her heart sank.

Of course. That would be all of the servants. The whole household would be turned out to greet their new mistress, no doubt shivering and stamping their feet in the cold, thinking of all the chores that were not getting done while they waited on her Grace's convenience, and quietly cursing her.

"There's no need to keep the servants from their work." Marina said, her voice small. "You didn't have to drag them all outside in this weather. It looks like rain."

The Duke glanced sharply at her. "You're now Lady Marina Blackburn, the new Duchess of Brixham. They'll all want to meet you, and this is the best opportunity for you to be introduced to everyone. It won't take more than five minutes, I promise."

Marina bit her lip. It was too late, anyway. The carriage rolled to a stop in front of Blackburn Manor, and she was impressed anew at its size and grandeur.

The Duke climbed out of the carriage first. He carefully handed down his mother, then reached up a hand to help Marina down.

The petty side of her wanted to ignore his hand, but the whole household – and Evelyn – were watching, and she didn't particularly want to cause a scene.

Marina took his hand and climbed down onto the raked gravel. His hand was warm, dry, and smooth, and a shiver rolled through her at his touch.

That, she reminded herself sternly, meant nothing. It was just because she was cold and the Duke's hand was warm, and that was all there was to it.

The wind blew powerfully across the top of the hill, whipping Marina's hair out of the careful style Louisa had wrestled it into, and stirring her stiff skirts around her legs. She shivered, already missing the warm, fur-lined interior of the Duke's carriage.

Not just his carriage anymore, Marina told herself. It's mine, now.

The Duke gestured towards the double row of servants, all turning to stare inquisitively at Marina.

She fought the urge to leap back into the carriage and pull down the blinds.

"I'll introduce you." the Duke said shortly, jerking his chin to indicate that she should walk along with him.

"My bags..."

"They will be unpacked and delivered to your room." He said firmly, and Marina blushed.

The Duke walked slowly along the lines of servants, introducing most of them by name. They all bobbed curtseys and made bows as Marina went past, smiling nervously.

She passed scullery maids, stable boys, kitchen-maids, house-maids, gardeners, under-gardeners, grooms, footmen, and more. The names and positions all blurred into one in Marina's mind. Even before Samuel had lost all of their money, they hadn't had half as many servants as this. What did all of these people find to do all day.

"This is Mrs. Robin, the cook." The Duke said, stepping onto the half-circle of a stone porch in front of the large front door. "I believe my mother has already sung her praises."

Mrs. Robin was a surprisingly young woman for a cook, and not at all like the pudgy, round-faced, red-cheeked middle-aged woman that Marina had imagined. She was a frighteningly tall and lanky woman of about thirty, with a fresh face and wisps of blonde hair escaping from under her cap.

She made an awkward curtsey, as if her limbs were too long and unwieldy for her to do anything with.

"It's a pleasure, your Grace." She said, flashing a smile.

"I'm pleased to meet you, Mrs. Robin."

The final two servants – and of course, the most important – were an essay in opposites.

The woman was short, barely five feet tall, and almost as round as she was tall. She was around fifty, with a beaming, good-natured face, and grey hair neatly pinned back into a bun.

The man was about five years younger, and was tall, thin, and serious.

"This is Mr. and Mrs.Turner, our butler and housekeeper respectively." The Duke said, flashing them both a smile. "They've worked for us for decades, and married seven years ago – a lovely occasion, was it not, Turner?"

"Certainly, your Grace." The butler replied, his tone as serious and grim as his face.

"We usually refer to Mrs.Turner as Mrs. Avery, to avoid confusion." Evelyn put in.

Mrs. Avery beamed at Marina. "If I may say, your Grace, you're an exceptionally beautiful young woman. I'd like to congratulate both of your Graces on your good fortune."

"And so would I." Sixsmith put in. They bowed and curtseyed in perfect unison, and Marina managed a weak smile.

"Thank you, all of you. It's a pleasure to make your acquaintance." Marina said, trying to direct her words to the whole household.

Then finally – finally – the introductions were over, and Marina could step inside the house.

It wasn't much warmer inside than outside, although at least she was sheltered from the wind. Marina found herself shivering uncontrollably. To make matters worse, tears were pricking at the inside of her eyes. She tried her best to blink them away.

"Marina, dear, are you ready for luncheon now?" Evelyn asked, and Marina's stomach clenched.

"I..." she managed, not sure that she could trust herself to keep talking.

Evelyn paused, eyeing her closely. "Are you quite alright?"

"I feel a little... tired, I think. From the journey."

"Ah." Evelyn nodded knowingly. "I often don't have much of an appetite after long carriage journeys. I do apologise, my dear. The luncheon will wait if you want to go on up to your room and take some time to rest."

Marina wanted to sag with relief. "Would you mind? That would be wonderful, thank you."

"No need to mention it, dear."

"That would work nicely for me." The Duke said brusquely, stripping off his coat, hat, and scarf and handing them to a footman. "I have work to do, and I'd be pleased to retire to my study for a while."

Evelyn gave a little moue of disapproval. "If you must, Adam, but I'm sure your new wife would appreciate your company."

The Duke's gaze flicked briefly to Marina.

"I'm sure her Grace can keep herself occupied and would be glad to have some time to rest."

He turned to stride away down the corridor, but Marina found herself speaking.

"Marina."

He paused, glancing over his shoulder.

"I beg your pardon."

She sucked in a breath. "My name is Marina, your Grace. I'm your wife, not a guest. We may as well not stand on ceremony now."

He eyed her for a long moment, his expression unreadable.

"Very well. My name is Adam, as you may have guessed. Feel free to use it."

Then he was gone, striding away from the hallway, his boot heels clicking on the stone.

Marina let out a breath she hadn't realized that she was holding.

"Where should I go, Evelyn?"

"Well, we've chosen a ladies' maid for you, and she'll escort you to your room."

A blank-faced young woman with vivid brown eyes and black hair peeking out from under her cap materialized behind Marina and indicated that she should follow her up the stairs.

Marina was too tired to ask questions.

The plush, red-carpeted stairs muffled their footsteps, spreading out from the circular landing like the spokes of a wheel. Marina found herself wondering where the other hallways led.

There was no time to find out, as the silent maid picked one of the hallways and scurried away down it, leaving Marina to follow.

They passed door after door, all closed, all identical, and took several twists and turns until Marina began to despair of ever finding her way out of this maze. Abruptly, the maid stopped at a room labelled The Hyacinth Room, and gestured for Marina to step through the door.

She found herself in a vast, plush room, with thick lavender carpets, rich purple-and-pink patterned wallpaper, and an ornate bed layered with blankets and pillows in a deep indigo. The curtains, heavy and velvet, were of a deep purple, almost black, fringed with gold tassels.

The overall effect was an impressive one. Purple was not Marina's favourite colour, but the shades complimented each other perfectly, giving an elegant look to the room that was simultaneously not overwhelming. She didn't feel as though she were drowning in purple.

"This is very beautiful." Marina remarked.

The maid's eyebrows shot up, and Marina wondered whether she ought to have been more careless about the opulence around her.

After all, she was a duchess now.

"I'll bring you up a tray of tea and refreshments, your Grace." The maid said mildly. It was the first time she'd spoken at all, and her voice was tinged with an accent that could have been French. "In the meantime, make yourself comfortable."

"I will." Marina replied, forcing a smile. As promised, her bags and suitcases were piled neatly in a corner.

The maid slipped out, closing the door softly behind her. Marina wandered over to the bed, running her palm over the whisper-soft covers.

Then she flung herself face down onto the bed and burst into tears.

Chapter Fifteen

Adam poured himself a generous amount of brandy and took a sip.

He usually didn't tend to drink alcohol so early in the day – it was a slippery slope that he'd seen far too many acquaintances and colleagues go tumbling down – but today was of course an exception.

Today was his wedding day.

It was mind-boggling to think that he was now a married man, with a brand-new wife upstairs, probably eyeing the expensive furnishings and deciding that she'd made a good choice after all.

No, that wasn't fair. Marina didn't strike him as that sort of young woman. She'd offered to marry him because he could relieve her father of his debt, not because he was a duke. In another woman, it would look like posturing, but not with Marina.

She was pretty, that was for sure. Kind, he'd noticed that. Evelyn seemed to like her already, and Marina warmed up around her.

She's better than I deserve, Adam thought bleakly. She's probably aware of that herself.

Adam slouched into his chair, swirling the brandy around his glass. He watched the amber liquid sparkle, then set it down on the desk. He had work to do and needed a clear head.

As the days progressed, no doubt Marina would find a place in the manor that would be "hers". Evelyn had requisitioned the morning room – the nicest one, that enjoyed pleasant sunlight for most of the day – and Adam had his study. It was an unspoken rule that they weren't disturbed in "their" rooms, not unless it was important.

Adam didn't even let the servants in to clean very often. There'd been an incident where a maid had upset a vast pile of papers while she was trying to dust a shelf. It was an accident, of course, and the girl didn't get into trouble, but it took Adam hours to reorganize the papers. Not ideal, really.

As a result, dust motes danced freely in the air, illuminated by beams of early afternoon light. Marina hadn't appeared yet, so he'd assumed that the luncheon would be relegated to suppertime.

Adam allowed himself another two minutes of sitting in silence, then reluctantly turned to the pile of letters and papers awaiting his attention.

The work never ended, did it?

The topmost letter – no doubt placed on top by the ever-thoughtful Turner, who would have recognized the handwriting – was from Matthew.

Adam sighed and reached out for the letter.

Matthew was currently at Brixham Hall, their countryseat. It was a substantial trip from here, and it wasn't ideal for Adam to trek back and forth. He was privately relieved to get Matthew out of the way for the wedding. What would Marina think of Matthew? What would he think of her?

Refusing to allow himself to think anymore of Marina – she was hardly important to any of this, he reminded himself – Adam tore open the letter and began to decipher Matthew's spidery handwriting.

Your Grace,

Allow me to offer congratulations on your impending nuptials. No doubt the happy event will have taken place by the time my correspondence arrives.

I have arrived at the countryseat of Brixham Hall, and I am dismayed to convey that all is not well here.

The overseer has neglected his responsibilities shockingly. I have been afraid that this would happen – if you recall, I advised against hiring that man in particular. Many of the tenants' rents are overdue, and they now have a great deal of back-paid rent owing. Naturally, the tenants are unable and unwilling to pay this rent. As far as I can gather, they did pay the rent, and it was pocketed by the overseer. I have of course dismissed the man.

As to recovering the funds owing, I am not able to do so without evicting all the tenants. I did not think you would agree with that course of action, and they are, after not, to blame.

I must urge you to travel down to Brixham Hall immediately to deal with this issue. If you wish to cancel the money owing, that must be done by you yourself, in person.

I reiterate, your presence is requested urgently at Brixham Hall, otherwise I will need to straighten out these problems myself. The only option open to me is to evict the tenants in order to pay the rent owing.

Do send me a note with your decision. I await your instructions.

Your Obedient Servant,

Matthew Harbinger

Adam bit off a curse.

He did remember Matthew advising against the overseer in question. But then, Adam had been in a hurry, keen to get back to London, and simply wanted somebody to manage his country estate in his absence. He'd dismissed Matthew's warnings, and now look at what had happened.

There was no information as to the amount owed by the unfortunate tenants – who'd clearly been swindled – or whether they would press charges against the overseer. It was possible that his theft couldn't be proved, but Matthew's instincts were worth listening to.

What was more, he had a good point. As a steward, Matthew could not cancel debts owing to his master, no matter how much he wished to. To recover the money, he would have to evict the tenants.

Of course, Adam wouldn't allow that to happen. There was nothing for it, he'd have to go.

Sighing to himself, he moved over to the bell pull, and hauled on it.

Turner appeared half a minute later, standing quietly in the doorway.

"Your Grace?"

"Pack my things, Turner. I'm going down to Brixham Hall."

Turner was too well-trained to display any surprise, although he would certainly be thinking it.

"Very well, your Grace. Shall I order her Grace's things to be prepared, too?"

"No, that won't be necessary." Adam said, bending over the stack of papers on the desk. "It's a business trip, I'm afraid. Unexpected, but nothing exciting."

"Very well, your Grace. How soon do you expect to leave? Shall I also prepare the carriage?"

Adam considered, chewing his lip.

"I won't leave tonight. Tomorrow morning, I think. That way, we'll arrive by nightfall. What do you think?"

"Very advisable, your Grace. I shall make the preparations at once."

Turner bowed and retreated. Adam sank down into his seat, pulling out documents and looking them over. He scribbled hasty replies, informing those who needed to know that he would be out of town for some time.

He hoped that the business would be concluded quickly. The idea of a long, complex case stretching out before him did not appeal.

Still, Adam already knew that he would cancel the "debt" that the tenants owed. It was the simplest thing to do. His tenants were not greedy, lavish nobles, who lived to excess and borrowed beyond their means. No, his tenants were good, hard working people, who hadn't borrowed money at all, and had only come to owe money because of one man's greed.

If anyone deserved to have their debts cancelled, it was those people.

Then the door flung open, and Evelyn stalked in.

"Do come in, Mother." Adam said, not looking up.

"Did I hear correctly that you are leaving for Brixham Hall tomorrow?" Evelyn demanded.

Adam sighed. "Who told you, Mother? I doubt it was Turner. One of the footmen? One of the maids? You've filled my household with spies."

"This is not funny, Adam, and I'd thank you to take it

seriously. Stop writing and listen to me."

Adam bit his lip. He replaced his pen and sat back in his seat.

"Very well. Yes, Mother, I am leaving for Brixham Hall. It's sudden and unexpected, and more than a little aggravating. I have a problem with my overseer, and Matthew wants me to go as soon as I can."

Evelyn placed her hands on her hips. "Well, this is very unkind, I must say."

"I did not plan it this way, Mother."

"I know, I know, but poor Marina had barely had time to settle in. I can't say I fancy a trek across to the country myself. It's not fair to make her move away from her friends and family so quickly."

Adam raised an eyebrow. "Yes, it would be unfair. That's why I am not going to do it."

There was a little silence at that.

"I beg your pardon?" Evelyn said, her voice deceptively quiet.

He raked a hand through his hair, noting the first warning throbs of a

headache at his temples. Wonderful.

"Marina is not coming with me, Mother. She'll remain here. I'm sure she'd prefer that. There's plenty to do in town, and she'll have you for company. I daresay she'll be entirely happy."

Evelyn moved forward, leaning down to rest her hands on the edge of Adam's desk, so as to better look him in the eyes.

"Adam, I came here to tell you that as a married man, you ought to be behaving very, very differently to the way you are now." she said, her voice cold and disapproving. "You barely spoke a word to your poor bride in the carriage, and you hared off to your study the moment you returned home. This is your wife, Adam! And now you plan to leave for the country, without her, for goodness only knows how long. Do you truly not see that this is unacceptable?"

Adam ground his teeth. "Yes, Mother, I am aware that she is my wife. She'll be treated with every courtesy, and every respect. I have no intention of curbing her freedom, so long as she does not humiliate me in public. Do you think she's desperate for my company at the moment? As far as I know, she's still in her room."

Evelyn chewed the inside of her cheek. "She is," she admitted. "I went up to check on her. That French ladies' maid we hired for her came up with a tea tray, and found the poor girl fast asleep, fully clothed. She's exhausted, poor lamb. I doubt she'll stir much for an hour or two, then back to bed. You can't drag her across the country now, Adam."

Adam wanted to tear his hair out in frustration. "I don't intend to, Mother. That is why I'm leaving her here. It's kinder. She can get used to the place, and to her new position, and I can deal with whatever nonsense is going on over at Brixham Hall. It's perfect."

Evelyn shook her head. "No, I'm afraid not. You can't possibly leave the day after your wedding, Adam."

"It's not a discussion. I'm going."

"Then you must take Marina with you. You wanted to marry, Adam. You need to think of how things look. A groom running off to his countryseat the day after his wedding, without his bride, looks like a man unhappy and dissatisfied. It would make the couple look like a laughing-stock, an ill-matched pair who can't stand each other's company. Is that what you want?

"I don't care about the opinions Society has of me." Adam snapped.

Evelyn didn't miss a beat. "But do you care about Marina's opinions of you?"

Adam hesitated. He wanted to say no, certainly not, he couldn't care less. But he realized, with a flash of annoyance, that it was not true. He did care about Marina's opinions. There was something about her that made him want to see her smile – smile at him – and maybe even laugh at something he said. The idea of thinking that he was an awful, cold-hearted man made him feel uncomfortable inside.

It was a similar sort of feeling he experienced when Evelyn disapproved of him. Nobody wanted to disappoint their mothers, after all.

There was really only one solution, and Adam was going to have to embrace it ungraciously.

"Fine." He snapped. "Marina can come with me. I have to go,

Mother, and if I can't leave her behind then she will have to come with me. Are you happy now? I daresay she'll be disappointed."

Evelyn pursed her lips, standing back.

"That's hardly the point."

"Isn't it? I thought your aim here was to preserve the new Duchess of Brixham's pride."

Evelyn rolled her eyes. "Don't be childish, Adam. You must see that I'm right."

He did see that but wasn't about to admit it.

I'd hoped that some distance between myself and Marina would help me think more clearly, Adam thought, *She's muddling my thoughts something terrible.*

And then, he was horrified to acknowledge that the woman was muddling his thoughts.

It'll all in your imagination. You haven't had a pretty young woman in the house since – well, ever. It's natural that it might throw you off balance a little. You'll get over this. Yours is a marriage of convenience, remember? That's what everybody wanted, after all.

Adam leaned back in his seat, clearing his throat.

"Well, you've gotten your way, Mother. Will you be coming with us?"

A strangely mischievous look crossed Evelyn's face, one that Adam did not like at all.

"I might join you later. For now, I have far too much to do here in London."

Adam fought not to roll his eyes.

"Oh, I see how it is, Mother."

Evelyn gave a dainty shrug, and left the room, closing the door behind her. Adam was left alone, to stew in irritation. He'd hoped to use the carriage ride to Brixham Hall to go over some of his work. There were debtors he needed to visit, but of course now he'd have to write to them instead.

Letters weren't as frightening as a personal visit.

No matter how hard he tried to concentrate on his work, Marina was still there in the back of his mind, watching him with that haunting, unreadable expression on his face, as if she could hear everything he was thinking.

That wasn't a reassuring thought. Not at all.

Chapter Sixteen

Somebody swept back the curtains, letting bright morning sunlight flood into the room.

Marina groaned, pressing her face into the pillow.

What time was it, and who had woken her up? She was used to being able to sleep in as late as she liked. The servants at home were far too busy to come and wake up their lazy employers on a morning.

"Good morning, your Grace." Came an unfamiliar voice, gently accented with a tinge of French. "It's time to wake up."

In a rush, everything came flooding back to Marina's memory. The wedding, the awkward carriage ride, the uninviting grandeur of Blackburn Manor, and the way she'd cried herself to sleep in her plush new bedroom.

Evelyn.

Adam. Her husband.

She sat bolt upright, vaguely remembering being badgered out of bed sometime in the evening, stripped out of her wedding gown, and placed into an unfamiliar yet undeniably comfortable nightgown. She was now in the bed, with plumped up pillows all around her, and layers of blankets.

The maid from yesterday stood serenely at the foot of the bed, holding a breakfast-tray in her hands.

"I'm sorry to wake you so early, your Grace." She said, "But the Dowager Duchess instructed it."

"Of course, of course." Marina managed, wiping sleep from her eyes. How long had she slept? It was hard to believe that she'd slept all through the afternoon and through the night. It was early in the morning, judging by the pink-streaked sky outside. Dawn had only just settled, and Marina had to admit that she did feel well-rested.

There was no sign of Adam's things in here. That meant that this was going to be her room, and hers alone. That was a relief.

Marina pulled herself up into a more comfortable sitting position and was a little taken aback by the maid placing the breakfast tray over her lap, setting out the little legs so that it formed a table. She retreated a few steps, waiting patiently and attentively to see what Marina would need next.

Marina glanced nervously at the young woman, whose face was placid and revealed nothing.

"This looks delicious, thank you."

"I shall pass on your compliments to the cook, your Grace."

Just like that, the compliment bounced right off.

Marina eyed the tray. It was standard fare – an assortment of fruit, hot toast, butter, a selection of jams, boiled eggs, and a large plate of fried food. Bacon, sausages, eggs, and so on. There was a large glass of what looked like freshly squeezed orange juice, along with a cup of tea.

It looked delicious indeed, but there was no way she would eat all of it.

"By the way, I forgot to ask last night. What is your name?" Marina asked, picking up a strawberry and biting into it.

There was just a fraction of a second of hesitation on the maid's part.

"My previous employers called me Jane, your Grace."

There was something about her tone that made Marina paused.

"Is... is Jane your name?"

The maid pursed her lips. "It is not, but my employers felt like my real name was not a proper one for a servant. They thought that Jane or Mary were more appropriate choices."

Marina let out a burst of laughter. "They changed your name?"

The maid did not laugh. "It is common practice is grand households, your Grace. For example, all of the footmen might be called James."

"But what if you wanted to speak to a specific footman?"

The maid shot her a pitying look.

"That would not happen, your Grace. One servant is very much like another. Any one will do."

Marina snorted. "Well, that's silly. Wait, his Gr – that is, Adam, my husband, he doesn't do that here, does he?"

"Not that I know of, your Grace."

"What is your name, then? Your real name, I mean, not what one of your employers thought ought to be your name."

She gave the tiniest of smiles. "My name is Geraldine, your

Grace."

Marina smiled back at her. "That's a lovely name. It's a pleasure to meet you, Geraldine."

The maid – Geraldine – favoured Marina with a wider smile.

"And you, your Grace. I am glad to be waiting upon you. I am trained as a ladies' maid and worked in Paris for a while."

"Really? You must tell me what Paris is like. I've never been."

"Of course, your Grace. But for now, I must pack for you."

Marina paused, a cup of tea halfway to her lips.

"Pack?"

A flash of uncertainty crossed Geraldine's face. "You... you did not know, your Grace?"

"Know what?"

Geraldine pressed her lips tightly together. "His Grace the Duke is leaving this morning for his country-seat. He is going to Brixham Hall."

Marina flinched at that. "Oh. Well. No, I didn't know that."

"You are to go with him. You are to leave after breakfast, and I am to go ahead with some of the other servants to prepare the hall for your stay."

Marina replaced her teacup with a clatter.

Nobody had told her about this. Admittedly, she had been asleep for most of the afternoon yesterday, but still.

"Right. Well. Nobody told me about this. Let's see what's going on here." Marina muttered, setting aside the breakfast tray and swinging her legs out of bed. She hurried across to the wardrobe, a little shocked to find her clothes already set out and hanging up neatly. When had Geraldine had time to do that?

It hardly mattered. She already had her shift on over her head by the time Geraldine gave a squawk and came rushing towards her.

"I am to help you dress, your Grace!"

"Oh. Sorry." Marina said, blushing. "I'm used to dressing myself."

Geraldine looked as if Marina had just confessed to never eating with a knife and fork in her life.

"When his Grace buys you finer dresses, you shall need my help to dress." Geraldine said severely.

"Of course, Geraldine. I do apologise." Marina said,

chastised.

***

"Evelyn. Evelyn!"

Marina scurried across the vast, echoing hallway and into the dining room. The door stood ajar, revealing Evelyn eating her breakfast by herself.

"Good morning, my dear!" Evelyn said, smiling. "I sent Geraldine to wake you early, I hope you don't mind. Did you sleep well?"

"What? Oh, yes, very well. The bed is extremely comfortable. But what's all this about going to Brixham Hall? Nobody said anything about that."

Evelyn's expression flickered. She dabbed her mouth with a napkin and got to her feet.

"Oh, that. It's very last minute, I do apologise. Adam has urgent, unavoidable business at his country-seat. Neither of us expected this, certainly not the day after your wedding. He must go, and he must go today. Of course, I was sure you'd want to go with him."

Marina pressed her lips together, not wanting to agree or disagree.

"It's just... well, I thought I would have more time to adjust."

A flash of pity crossed Evelyn's face. She reached out, taking both of Marina's hands in hers.

"I know, and I am sorry. It wasn't meant to happen like this. But Brixham Hall is lovely, and you'll get a taste of running your own home without an interfering mother-in-law in the way."

Marina forced a smile. "I don't think you'll be an interfering mother-in-law, Evelyn."

The other woman smiled sadly. "I hope not. I couldn't have asked for a nicer young woman to marry my son. I hope Adam knows how lucky he is. What's more..." she paused, glancing over her shoulder and dropping her voice. "He wasn't always like this, Marina. Just give him a chance. Give him time."

Marina frowned. "What do you mean, he wasn't always like

this?"

Evelyn opened her mouth to reply but closed it against at the sound of footsteps.

Adam appeared, dressing in a crisp, fresh travelling clothes, heels clicking on the polished floor. He glanced briefly between Evelyn and Marina.

"Good morning, Mother. Good morning, Marina. I trust you're all packed and ready to go?"

Evelyn let go of Marina's hands, stepping back. Marina drew in a breath and turned to face her brand-new husband.

"I believe Geraldine is getting my things ready. But Adam, I had no idea we were leaving so suddenly. I'm not prepared. I thought I'd have time to settle in."

He avoided her gaze. "I know, and I do apologise. I'd offer to let you stay behind, but my mother assures me that it's not the done thing at all for newlyweds to separate so suddenly. Of course, if you wish to stay, you can stay. I shan't force you come along with me."

Marina winced. "You have a point. I'd better go with you, I suppose. But what about my parents? I must visit them and say goodbye."

"I'm afraid there's no time." Adam said decisively. "I'm sorry, but I'd already planned to have gone by now. It's a long trip to Brixham Hall, so unless you want to travel in the dark, we need to leave soon."

"But, my family..."

"I suggest you write a note. Inform them of where we're going – Turner can provide you with the address – and they're even welcome to visit us, if they don't mind travelling. You may also write to them when we arrive at Brixham Hall. You'll find the post remarkably reliable."

And that was that. Adam turned on his heel and walked away down the hallway, leaving Marina and Evelyn standing alone.

She breathed out heavily and turned to face Evelyn.

"Where can I find writing paper and ink, please?" Marina asked, shakily.

***

Dear Mama, Papa, and Josephine

My husband, the Duke – his name is Adam, by the way – has sudden, urgent business at his country-seat. The place is called Brixham Hall, and I'm writing the address at the top of this note.

It's very sudden, and I was hoping to entertain visits from you all here, at Blackburn Manor, in the next few days.

Adam says that he won't force me to come along with him, but I'd be a laughing stock if I stayed behind. Newlyweds are supposed to stay together, after all.

I really haven't seen enough of Blackburn Manor to describe it to you, but it's very large and grand. Very pretty, too. My new mother-in-law, the Dowager Duchess, Lady Evelyn Blackburn, is a very pleasant woman, and has taken pains to make me feel welcome. I have my own maid, a Frenchwoman named Geraldine, who I like very much.

As to my husband, I get the feeling I will not see him very much. On the eve of our wedding day, he retreated to his study to complete some work.

I cannot decide if I am relieved or disappointed by that.

Marina paused, then crossed out the final sentence, carefully scratching it out so the words couldn't be read.

"Marina, we need to leave." Adam's voice echoed through the hallways, not quite demanding, but with a tinge of irritation.

She'd better write fast.

I'll finish this note here, as we have to leave soon. But I love you all very much, and I miss all three of you.

Love to you all.

Your loving daughter and sister,

Marina

P.S Although you may now refer to me as Her Grace, the Duchess of Brixham.

She finished the letter and folded it hastily. Turner was waiting in the hallway, and Marina handed him the letter.

"Will you post this, please?" she asked, breathlessly.

"Of course, your Grace. I shall have it delivered by the end of today." He answered, giving a light bow. "His Grace is waiting for you in the carriage."

Marina winced. She was late, then.

She hurried down the steps towards the carriage, spotting her own bags and boxes lashed to the roof.

She tumbled inside, and the footman closed the door after her.

Adam was already inside, as the butler had told her, sitting in the far corner from the door. He was staring out of the window and didn't glance at Marina as she made herself comfortable.

"I told you I wanted to leave immediately." He said, still not looking at her. "We'll have to travel the last mile or two in the dark, now."

She flushed. "I'm sorry, your Gr – Adam. I was writing a letter to my family."

"I told you to write a note."

She felt her temper surging. "Well, I didn't want to write a note, I wrote a letter. I miss my family very much, and I'd like to remind you that this trip is of your making, in any case."

She bit her lip, wishing desperately that she hadn't spoken so sharply.

Adam Blackburn could make her life very, very miserable if he wished.

He glanced her way, and she saw surprise written on his face before it was neatly smoothed away.

"Of course." He said, his tone smooth and calm. "I beg your pardon. I forgot that you were not informed of this last night."

The carriage lurched forward, wheels crunching on the immaculate gravel. Marina leaned forward, waving to Evelyn, who stood on the front steps waving goodbye.

The carriage picked up speed, leaving Blackburn Manor behind. Neatly raked gravel turned to uneven cobbles, but the carriage was so well-sprung it hardly rattled the occupants at all.

Marina leaned back in her seat and tried not to look at her husband on the other side of the carriage.

It struck her, possibly for the first time, that they were going to spend the rest of the day in this carriage, just the two of them.

No Evelyn to make things more comfortable. Even Geraldine had gone ahead.

Marina bit back a sigh and closed her eyes.

It was going to be a long journey.

She wished she'd brought a book.

Chapter Seventeen

Adam impassively watched the scenery flick by. He'd catalogued all the tasks he'd need to accomplish once he arrived. Matthew was nothing if not efficient, but there would still be plenty of work to be done.

He was exhausted already.

He'd planned to get a head start on his tasks as soon as he arrived, but Marina's late appearance put paid to that. It was annoying, but of course it wasn't really her fault.

She'd slept most of the day away yesterday, then on into the night. Adam had felt a twinge of worry at that. Surely it wasn't normal for a person to sleep that heavily? He'd considered calling the doctor, but Evelyn told him that she was just tired, and he ought to leave her alone.

He shot a quick glance in the direction of his new wife. Sure enough, she seemed wide-awake and comfortable, which was something of a relief.

Put yourself in her place. How would you like it, being torn away from your family and home just like that?

That was what Evelyn had said. Putting himself in the position of others wasn't something Adam was good at, nor something he cared to do.

But he assumed that Marina was feeling out of place, nervous, and unsettled.

That was fair enough.

He shot another glance her way, and this time she caught him looking.

Before, Marina had been leaning against the side of the carriage, watching the scenery go by. Now, she was looking straight at him, her expression curious.

Adam forced himself not to flinch or look away. That would look guilty, as though he ought not to have been stealing glances at her. He smiled politely, and turned back to the window, pleased with his self-control.

"How long do we have to go to get to Brixham?" Marina asked, breaking the silence.

Adam cleared his throat, resolutely not looking at her.

"Quite a way, I'm afraid."

"Oh. I wish I'd brought a book."

He glanced at her, frowning. "That is a pity. You ought to have brought something to occupy yourself. It's a long journey."

Marina blushed. The colour in her cheeks was shockingly becoming, and Adam deliberately forced his thoughts along another path.

"I know that." she replied shortly. "As I'm sure you know, we left in something of a hurry."

He sighed, picking at non-existent flecks of dust on his breeches.

So that was her game, then. This was why she was talking to him. Not because she was the slightest bit interested in him as a person, but because she was bored.

"There is a large library at Brixham Hall. You can help yourself to whatever books you like, although I would ask that you don't bring books back to Blackburn Manor without asking me first."

Marina brightened at that.

"Oh, exciting. I didn't have time to look through the library at Blackburn Manor. We have a library at home, although it's quite a small one, and mostly novels. I suppose you're the sort of man who doesn't approve of novels."

Adam suppressed a smile.

"Not at all. I quite enjoy a good novel. You'll find plenty at Brixham Hall, I can assure you. The collection belonged to my father, although he didn't spend much time reading them. I don't have much time these days, either."

Marina tilted her head to one side. "That's a pity. Reading is a wonderful pastime."

"I agree, and most improving. When I was a young boy, I'd spend hours and hours in there. The housekeeper now is the same woman who lived there when I was young, although she was just a maid then. She was a great reader, and more than once she was nearly caught reading the books she was meant to be dusting."

He paused, chuckling at a memory, and glanced up to find Marina watching him again, with a curious expression on her face.

"What stopped her from getting caught?" Marina said, with a tone that indicated she knew exactly how she'd avoided it.

Adam bit his lip. "Well, I happened to be around, and I kept whoever had come into the room talking until Emma was able to replace the book and look as though she were getting on with her chores. It's Mrs Brown now, of course."

"Of course." Marina echoed.

Adam turned back to the scenery, wishing he hadn't revealed such a private story. After all, Marina didn't care what he'd been like as a boy. She probably didn't care about anything except securing her family's safety and living a comfortable life.

And that was fair enough, Adam reminded himself. That was their deal, after all.

But he ought to stick to his end of the bargain and keep things neutral and business-like between them.

So, he resolutely kept his eyes on the scenery flashing by and tried to ignore Marina. She was still looking at him, he knew it.

"What's Mrs Brown like, then?" Marina said, apparently not getting the hint at all.

Adam pressed his lips together.

"She's a kind, clever, and efficient woman. She's about my mother's age, or possibly a little younger. I believe you'll like her."

"I'll ask her what sort of books she likes reading."

"I believe she prefers improving books." Adam heard himself say. "Not that she objects to a good novel, of course, but she always preferred informational books."

"Well, each to their own, I suppose. Personally, I love adventure stories. I do like novels, although sometimes they infuriate me. Have you read Pamela?"

"Virtue Rewarded? I don't believe I have, although I've seen the title in our library before."

Marina snorted, rolling her eyes. "It made me extremely angry. I'll explain why after you read it, although I'm sure you'll understand what's so awful about it."

Adam clenched his jaw. This journey was not going well. He'd intended to enjoy a peaceful trip to his countryside, not deal with Marina's endless chatter.

Of course, if he was honest with himself, the chatter wasn't what bothered him. Not one bit.

No, it was Marina herself. It felt as though every fibre of Adam's body was aware of her, in a way he'd never experienced before. It was thrilling and terrifying, and he was suddenly and shockingly aware of how small the carriage was, and how little space there was between them.

He cleared his throat, leaning a little closer to his side of the carriage.

"I'm afraid I won't have time to read it, I am very busy. We don't all have hours of free time every day." Adam said curtly, deliberately not looking her way.

He'd half expected tears at his sharp tone, or maybe a hurt little gasp. Marina huffed in annoyance and sat back against the carriage seat with a thump. When he risked a glance her way, she was looking out of the window again, her arms crossed against her chest.

"Yes, I'm sure you have so much more to do with your time than read books." Marina muttered. "Unlike me, who is now a lady of leisure and has nothing to do but wander around the house all day and be bored. I'm as thrilled at all this as you are."

Adam bit his lip.

"I didn't mean that."

"Yes, you did."

He sighed. "Being a lady – a duchess, even – is an odd sort of thing. There's more responsibility involved in the position, and more work, although simultaneously there's less that you'll need to do for yourself. I understand that you were quite active in the running of your household at all."

Marina was quiet for a moment.

"You could say that." she said, after a moment or two had passed. "But this is... this is different."

Adam shrugged, a casual gesture that his father had always disapproved of.

"You'll get used to it. People always get used to things. It's annoying, I know, but you'll adjust, probably more quickly than you think. I shouldn't worry."

He glanced at her again, and this time his breath caught in his throat.

Marina had her hands twisted together in her lap now, and she was staring down with a pensive expression on her face. Sunlight streamed in through the window, illuminating her profile in gold.

She was beautiful, more beautiful than Adam could have imagined.

He blinked hard, trying to remove the odd sort of glamour that had descended on the scene.

Control yourself, Adam. You've encountered beautiful women before.

In fact, he'd met women much more beautiful than Marina. That wasn't an insult of any sort, it was a simple fact, just like the fact that many men were more good-looking than Adam himself.

Not many in London Society, though, he had to admit.

So, what was it about Marina? What made his heart clench whenever he saw her? It was a strange and disconcerting thing, and he hadn't experienced it before.

It had happened the very first time they met, when Marina had come into the study to save her poor, weak-willed father from Adam. He remembered how she'd looked then, infused with righteous anger, fearless.

It was mesmerizing.

Then Marina glanced up, catching Adam staring at her, dumbfounded.

He hastily looked away, cursing himself for being such a fool.

Of course, it was hardly the worst thing in the world for a husband to find his wife attractive, even if their marriage was based on an arrangement of convenience. Marina was a pretty woman, and she was an interesting and clever one, too. There was no reason why he shouldn't enjoy her company – in moderation, of course – and admire her face and figure.

Not here, though, when they were going to be cramped together in a too-small carriage for goodness only knew how long.

Adam folded his arms over his chest and closed his eyes. Perhaps if he pretended to go to sleep, she would leave him alone.

"What books do you like, then?"

Marina, apparently, was not good at taking hints.

Adam sighed. "I'm trying to sleep."

"I'm just trying to make conversation. We've probably got hours yet to go."

"We do. And I'd like to spend those hours sleeping, if it's all the same to you." Adam responded sharply.

There was a moment of silence, then Marina gave a huff of

annoyance.

She didn't speak again, and Adam kept his eyes firmly shut.

Chapter Eighteen

"Marina, wake up. Wake up, we're here."

Unceremoniously jerked from a pleasant yet vague dream, Marina opened her eyes, bleary and disoriented.

They were still in the carriage, although night had fallen while she slept. That was an uncomfortable, jarring sort of sensation – falling asleep in broad daylight and waking up in the dark.

The carriage had stopped moving, too. After around six hours of constant but gentle movement, it felt odd to be sitting still.

Adam was sitting back in his seat. He'd obviously leaned over to shake her awake and was now pulling on a pair of gloves in a business-like manner.

She shuffled into a more upright position, wiping sleep from her eyes and peering out of the window.

After Adam had so firmly said that he wanted to rest – an obvious ploy to end the conversation – Marina had been left with nothing to do but try and rest herself.

Of course, after her long sleep the night before, she wasn't particularly tired. But between the absolute boredom, the warmth of the plush interior, and the gentle rocking movement of the carriage, she had inevitably fallen asleep.

Marina wished she hadn't. Between the grogginess from being so unceremoniously awoken, she had a headache forming at her temples, and felt uncomfortably rumpled and grubby.

Too late for that now, of course, because a footman was swinging open the carriage door. Marina's eyes adjusted to the dark, and she saw that beyond the immediate gloom, the sky was lit up by dozens of lanterns.

Adam stepped out first, turning neatly to offer his hand up to Marina.

She took it, more out of reflex than any real thought, and stepped down onto a gravel drive just as immaculately maintained as the drive back at Blackburn Manor.

"Well, here it is." Adam said, and she could have sworn that she'd heard a tinge of pride in his voice.

Marina inspected her new – second – home and found herself speechless yet again.

Like Blackburn Manor, Brixham Hall was a large, sprawling place, cleverly designed and well-maintained. A row of servants spread out from the front door, although thankfully there weren't quite as many as back at Blackburn.

Perhaps Marina was getting more used to it, because the sight of all those servants didn't fill her with dread.

There were dozens of cheerfully lit windows looking down on them. Light and warmth drifted from the open front door. Above, the sky was velvet-blue and dotted with little silvery stars. Marina estimated that the sun had gone down only an hour or two ago and regretted that she hadn't been awake to see it.

Adam cleared his throat beside her, and Marina realized that she'd been staring.

"Shall we?" he said, as polite and pleasant as a stranger.

"Of course." Marina responded automatically. He offered his hand again, but she pretended not to see it. Out of the corner of her eye, Marina saw Adam curl his hand into a fist and drop it down to his side, as if he were trying to hide the motion.

They walked side by side down the row of servants, with Adam making the introductions again. Marina's smile widened when she saw Geraldine at the very top of the stairs.

"I'm glad you made it here safely, Geraldine."

Geraldine smiled modestly. "Your rooms are all ready, your Grace. I think you will be very happy with them."

"I'm sure I will. Thank you."

They moved past to the final two people by the front door. One was a middle-aged woman with a beaming smile and greying brown hair, and the other was a shockingly young man of around twenty-nine, who appeared to be the butler. He boasted a head of red hair, carefully slicked back, and a well-featured face.

"This is Mrs Brown, the housekeeper, and Mr Julian, the butler."

Mrs Brown took a step forward, still smiling.

"It's a pleasure to meet you, your Grace. I'd like to offer my congratulations on your marriage."

Marina smiled. "Thank you, Mrs Brown. Adam mentioned you on the journey here, and I'm quite looking forward to meeting you. The house is beautiful, by the way."

Mrs Brown beamed, as if the compliment on the house was a personal compliment to her. Well, perhaps it was.

"I'm so glad you like it, your Grace. Perhaps once you've settled in, you might like a tour?"

"I would love one, thank you."

Mrs Brown gave a nod and a smile. "We've prepared dinner for an hour's time, as per your request, your Graces. I hope that's in order."

"That sounds wonderful, thank you, Mrs Brown." Adam said, smiling.

Marina couldn't help but stare at him. His smile was a wide, sincere one, that crinkled the corners of his eyes and made him look...

Well, Marina didn't want to think any more on that line of thought. It didn't concern her how handsome Adam may or may not look. It was nice that he seemed so fond of his housekeeper, though.

Footmen plodded to and from the carriage, bringing in heavy trunks and bandboxes, the ones that didn't need to go ahead with Geraldine and the other servants.

Marina stepped inside, more to get out of the way than anything else, and the servants shuffled past her, going about their day once again.

"I hope it isn't inconvenient for them, us arriving so late." Marina found herself saying to no one in particular.

Adam, who was in the process of pulling off his gloves, coat, and hat, paused.

"Well, probably not. After all, when I'm not here, they don't have much to do. Mrs Brown keeps the place going, but aside from the occasional spring-cleaning job, there isn't much for them to do. That's why the household here is much smaller than Blackburn."

"So I see." Marina replied, smiling uncomfortably. Was it her imagination, or was there a sort of tense atmosphere between herself and Adam? Nothing unpleasant, just... just strange. Like a magnetism.

No, it must just be her imagination. After all, she was very groggy.

Adam smiled tightly. "I shall go and change, and I'll meet you at dinner. Mrs Brown will give you a tour, if you like, although I'm quite hungry and I will start without you if you aren't at the dinner table in an hour."

Marina tilted her head. "Was that a joke?"

Adam blinked. "No. I really will start without you."

She suppressed a smile, shaking her head. Adam cleared his throat and strode past her, hurrying up the stairs.

Marina took a moment to look around. The front door opened directly into a circular, cavernous hall, with a marbled floor and a fantastic chandelier hanging from the ceiling. It was hard to tell at this time of night, of course, but she guessed that the place would be remarkably well-lit in the daytime.

A curving staircase swooped up to a first-floor landing, which was richly carpeted and decorated with an ornate carved banister.

The foyer broke off into two hallways, along which various doors opened. There were antique seats and various expensive-looking trinkets placed on tables along the hallways.

Marina decided that she would explore the hallways later. For now, she wanted to change out of her travel-worn clothes and into something else. Adam's comment about how hungry he was had sparked her stomach into rumbling.

She hurried up the staircase, the plush carpet muffling her footsteps. On the landing, there were two ways to go. Two identical, red-carpeted hallways sprang away in different directions. Marina paused, nibbling her lip and glancing down each one.

Where was her room? Geraldine knew where it was, but obviously Geraldine had gone ahead. Should she just wander down the hallways in turn, opening each door as she came to it?

No, that was a bad idea. She might well open a door into Adam's room and catch him in a state of undress.

That thought sent a flush of heat to Marina's cheeks, no matter how firmly she told herself to calm down.

"You are in the west wing, your Grace."

She flinched at the cool, collected voice, and turned to see Mrs Brown standing behind her.

"Oh. It's you, Mrs Brown you gave me quite a start, I didn't hear you coming."

Mrs Brown chuckled. "I do apologise. I took the servants'

staircase, which brings you out just along the hall. His Grace suggested that you be put in the west wing, as that side of the house affords the finest views. He is retiring to his childhood room, on the east wing."

Marina bit her lip. She wished Adam hadn't explained just how separate their rooms would be. Of course, the servants would have found out anyway, but still.

"Shall I escort you to your room? This house is something of a maze, I'm afraid."

Marina smiled in relief. "I'd like that, thank you."

"You'll get used to it, of course."

Mrs Brown led the way down the left-hand hallway, stopping at a large, white-painted wooden door, and gestured for Marina to go in.

"Thank you, Mrs Brown." Marina said, pausing at the doorway.

The housekeeper's face was shadowed in the gloom, and Marina couldn't help but remember what Adam had said about he and Mrs Brown reading together in the library. Did she look on him as a son, or a younger brother? If so, she would be naturally protective over him.

"It's no trouble at all, your Grace." Mrs Brown replied smoothly and sailed away down the hallway.

That left Marina alone to discover her new room.

She pushed open the door to find Geraldine already there, taking out an emerald-green gown that Marina did not recognize.

The room itself was fabulous, of course. The thick, white carpet was even deeper than the hallways, and the walls were painted white, too. The room was saved from being glaringly bright and sterile by the endless pops of colour – a teal blue bedspread with matching curtains, red-and-white curtains at the windows, and colourful paintings on the walls.

Perhaps Marina could take in more details when she wasn't so tired. For now, however, she was distracted by the dress Geraldine had laid out. She spotted a fashion magazine on the dressing-table, opened at an instruction page for a shockingly complicated hairstyle.

Geraldine beamed at Marina.

"I thought we could try something different tonight, your

Grace."

Marina wanted nothing more than to wear something comfortable and simple, and maybe just to leave her hair as it was.

But Geraldine looked so very excited.

"Alright." Marina said, smiling back. "Let's try it, then."

Chapter Nineteen

Adam needn't have worried about Marina arriving late.

He'd barely taken his own seat before he heard the rustle of taffeta skirts against the staircase. Much as he hated his own reaction, Adam sucked in a sharp breath, and craned his neck to watch Marina's entrance into the dining room.

He wasn't disappointed.

She wore one of the dresses he'd bought for her as a wedding present – Adam doubted that she even knew he'd bought them for her – and the effect was truly breath-taking.

The dress was a shade of emerald green, with ruffles and swathes of lace around the sleeves and bodice. It was no doubt a showier affair than Marina might have chosen for herself, but the expensive style and fit suited her to a tee. The colour was perfect for her, making her eyes glow in the candlelight.

Her hair was done differently too, piled on top of her head in a waterfall of carefully constructed braids and ribbons. Tiny green glass flowers blinked out from the depths of her smooth, glossy locks, catching the light when she moved her head.

With a shock, Adam realized that she was talking to him.

"Do you like it?"

Marina was watching him watch her, her head tilted to one side, assessing.

Was there a hint of uncertainty in her voice? No, there couldn't be. She looked too fine and confident in that gown not to be sure of herself.

"It's very pretty. I like the colour." Adam managed.

Somehow, I like the colour didn't seem to cut it. He shifted uncomfortably in his chair, not enjoying the way his gaze was so often drawn to Marina.

He'd chosen the gown for its pretty colour. Adam had no idea what young ladies liked when it came to gowns and fashion. He'd suggested to his mother that he should simply finance Marina's choices and let her choose gowns for herself. Then she'd be sure of buying things that she liked.

But Evelyn tutted and said that there would be plenty of

time for her to buy her own things as their marriage progressed, and a new husband ought to buy gifts for his wife.

And so, Adam had simply walked into a modiste, and picked out various fabrics, matching them up to dress styles in the magazine they offered. Shortly afterwards, the dresses were ready, as if by magic. He barely remembered commissioning this one.

And yet, he couldn't take his eyes away from Marina. That led to the uncomfortable truth that it wasn't the dress that took his breath away, but Marina.

He cleared his throat, forcing himself to look at the fabulous array of food set out before them.

"Mrs Brown has really outdone herself." He said, his voice small and tinny in the large room. He wished that the dining room at Brixham Hall wasn't quite so large. Or better yet, that he was dining alone. He wouldn't be tortured by these uncomfortable sensations if Marina was not here, after all.

Probably.

"Yes, this looks delicious." Marina said, strolling down the length of the dining table to take a seat directly beside him. "Let's eat, then."

***

Marina's stomach rumbled appreciatively. It had been something of a struggle to get Geraldine to hold back on drawing in the corset – she seemed to be of the opinion that a lady's waist should be a ridiculously tiny thing – but Marina had won that battle, at least.

Other ladies could have tiny waists if they want. Marina had organs to house in there. What was more, she was hungry, and was going to need room for food.

She sat down beside Adam, who'd naturally taken a place at the head of the table, and smiled at the footman filling up her glass with wine.

"Do tell Mrs Brown thank you, won't you?"

The footman looked mildly horrified at being directly addressed, but managed to bow without spilling the wine, and backed hastily away.

Adam snorted.

"Steady on, you haven't even tried the food yet."

"Well, it smells delicious." Marina said firmly. "I can't wait."

Adam shifted in his seat again. He was doing that a lot, Marina noticed. He also seemed to be avoiding looking at her, which was quite a feat considering that they were the only people at the dinner table.

"You don't need to sit directly beside me, you know." he said, a tad too sharply.

Colour rose to Marina's face. She saw one of the footmen shoot a sidelong look at his companion. Marina cleared her throat.

"I don't think we need to be waited on while we eat, do you, Adam?"

Adam shrugged, then winced and rolled his shoulders, as if regretted
shrugging at all.

"If you prefer. I certainly don't mind."

"Excellent."

Marina made eye contact with Julian, who was hovering expectantly in the corner.

"As you wish, your Graces." He said smoothly and gestured to the rest of the footmen.

The servants obediently filed out, closing the door softly behind them.

Then Marina and Adam were alone.

"Why should I not sit beside you?" Marina asked, her voice low. "Would you rather I sit at the opposite end of the table, so that we can pretend that we don't know each other?"

Adam pursed his lips. He did that when he was annoyed, she noticed.

"Don't be argumentative, Marina. I just thought that perhaps you might like to read or entertain yourself some other way. You don't need to talk to me."

She rolled her eyes. "I'm too tired to read, and I have a headache. Don't worry, you needn't talk to me if you don't want to, but I'd appreciate it if you didn't let the servants know just how boring you find my company."

He at least had the grace to blush.

"I did not mean that. I'm tired, just like you, and I spoke out of turn. But, really, is there anything preventing us from starting as we mean to go on? I'm sure you intend to lead your own life, and I'll lead mine."

Marina filled her plate deftly from the bowls and plates of food set out. There was nothing groundbreaking in the food – meat, vegetables, potatoes, bread, cheese, and some fish – but she was starvingly hungry and it was all cooked to perfection.

"I thought we agreed that we'd be friends at least." She remarked.

A muscle jumped in Adam's jaw. He still wasn't looking at her, and for some reason, that bothered Marina. She felt like slamming her palms down on the table and bellowing into his face.

"Look at me, Adam! Really look at me!"

He'd looked at her when she first walked into the room, trussed up in that admittedly marvellous dress and the ridiculous ringlets Geraldine had forced her hair into.

For a moment, Marina had been sure that she saw admiration in his gaze, even awe.

Then it was gone, and she felt foolish for ever thinking that it was there in first place. Adam was the Duke of Brixham, after all. He must be very familiar with beautiful young women.

More beautiful than me, of course, Marina reminded herself.

She cleared her throat, glancing at him again.

"So, what do you intend to do tomorrow?"

The muscle jumped again in Adam's jaw.

"Marina, you ought to know that I'm going to be tremendously busy during all the time we're here. I'm sorry to disappoint you – if indeed you are disappointed – but you and I really won't be spending time together. I have a great deal of work to do. This isn't a holiday for me. Of course, I have no objections to you spending your time however you would like. You'll have money, and horses, and the carriage at your disposal. You may go where you like, whenever you like. But please don't bother me while I'm working. My business is very important to me."

Marina was sure that her face was going an interesting shade of scarlet.

That would almost certainly clash with the vivid green of her dress. She glanced down at her plate, which now looked ridiculously overfilled and much less appetizing than before.

"I see." She said, ignoring the sudden nausea welling up inside her. "I am so sorry to inconvenience you in this way."

Adam was looking at her now. She could see him out of the corner of her eye, watching her nervously. He thought he'd hurt her feelings.

Well, he has, Marina thought, with a surge of rage.

She got to her feet, pushing back her chair. It wobbled but didn't fall back with a crash. She was relieved at that. It would be too embarrassing to have the footmen run in while they were having an argument.

Adam blinked, a little taken aback.

"Marina, please just sit down. I'm sorry if this has upset you, but I needed to be plain."

"Don't worry. You've made yourself very plain. I think I ought to have stayed in London, don't you? It's too late now, of course."

Marina turned on her heel, striding out of the room. The ridiculous skirts on her ridiculous dress kept catching on the sides of the ridiculous chairs.

"Marina!"

She didn't turn back.

Marina stepped out into the hallway and closed the door softly behind her. She wanted to slam it, but that would be childish and would possibly bring the servants running.

She waited for a moment, not sure whether Adam would come out after her.

She wasn't sure if she wanted him to or not.

It occurred to Marina that she couldn't go back to her room. Geraldine would be there, tidying and putting clothes away, and she would want to know why Marina was back so soon. There were no doubt endless parlours and morning rooms and places for Marina to hide, but she didn't know where they were yet.

Marina sank down onto a seat in the hallway and burst into tears. Thankfully, nobody was around to see her, so she indulged in tears for a moment or two, before angrily wiping them away.

Just my luck, Marina thought mournfully. I don't know what I expected. I knew what he was like before I met him, but I suppose I didn't think that his heart was this ice cold.

It was a valuable lesson, she supposed.

As she sat there, Marina's stomach continued to rumble, much to her annoyance.

Chapter Twenty

Adam drummed his fingers on his desk, eyeing the papers Matthew had set out before him.

"This is a mess." He said at last.

Matthew inclined his head. "Very much so, your Grace. I suggest that you visit the tenants as soon as possible, to smooth ruffled feelings and buy us a little more time to unravel this matter."

Adam sighed. "I'd rather not."

Matthew pursed his lips and said nothing. There was nothing to say. Adam knew that he had to visit his tenants, and Matthew knew that he knew that.

The problem was that these tenants were too familiar with the old Duke. Adam could feel their eyes on him, weighing him up, assessing, cataloguing his flaws. It felt that here, in Brixham, the old Duke's influence was much more concentrated. In Blackburn, the delights of London were close enough that Adam felt more at home and less under his father's shadow. He'd been staying in Blackburn Manor when he first became duke in any case, and that seemed to count for something.

To make matters worse, Adam's stomach chose to break the silence by giving out a determined, lengthy rumble.

Matthew's eyebrows flickered. If Adam had been a blushing sort of man, he'd have turned beetroot red.

"I do beg your pardon." He said smoothly. "I missed breakfast this morning."

He'd taken the cowardly way out. There'd been no sign of Marina since their disastrous dinner last night, and Adam was struggling to assuage his guilt. It wasn't his fault that she expected attention from him that he'd been clear that he could not give.

Adam cleared his throat, ignoring the reproachful voice at the back of his mind that sounded too much like his mother.

"I can fetch you a plate of food if you like, your Grace." Matthew said smoothly.

"No, thank you. I haven't time to eat. There's too much to do."

Adam glanced up to find Matthew's eyes on him, thoughtful

and assessing.

"The old Duke used to say that too, your Grace. It was also his custom not to interact with his tenants. He believed it was beneath him as a duke and was solely my responsibility."

Now Adam was going red.

"I don't believe that. That is, that's not my custom."

"I didn't mean that it was, your Grace. I only meant to hint that perhaps changing times require changing approaches. Your tenants are fond of you, and you have greatly lessened the burdens placed upon them by the old Duke. Perhaps a visit is in order, after all."

Adam drummed his fingers on the desk again. He stopped and felt the pads of his fingers starting to sting. He had to learn to work out his anxiety in a more wholesome manner, and not beat tattoos into the desk and wear the flesh from his fingers.

"Saddle up my horse." Adam said at last. "And a horse for you, too. We'll go out tomorrow, when this rain has cleared up."

"Of course, your Grace." Matthew made a neat bow. "Is there anything else?"

"Yes, actually. Prepare a list of tenants for me to visit. I'd like to make my presence felt, and I'm keen to meet as many as possible. However, let's prioritise tenants who are directly affected by this problem. What do you think?"

"That is an excellent notion, your Grace. I can think of at least a dozen families who would benefit from your visit. Perhaps a public address might also be in order?"

Adam cringed at the thought of publicly addressing a crowd of stone-faced tenants but forced himself to nod.

This was what being a duke was all about, in any case.

"Yes, very good, Matthew."

Matthew bowed neatly again, and slunk out of the room, leaving Adam alone in his study.

He sat for a moment or two, considering.

He'd better change into his riding things. Adam pushed back his chair and got up with a sigh, striding out into the hallway.

He was passing the half-open library door when he heard his name spoken.

Adam froze.

"Yes, his Grace was always in here when he was young.

Always. I think he must have read every book on the shelves, at least twice."

That was Mrs Brown. Adam hovered by the door, peeking through the opening.

He could see Mrs Brown standing by the window seats, talking to Marina. Both women held a book in their hands and seemed to be comparing them.

Marina was wearing a plain grey gown, simple but becoming, and her hair swept back in a knot at the nape of her neck. Two corkscrew curls escaped at either side of her temples, almost brushing her collarbone.

She looked beautiful. She looked elegant and effortless in a way that made Adam's heart clench inside him, and he didn't know why. She was going to be a wonderful duchess, that much was clear.

Adam knew that his servants were already taking to her. She was kind, attentive, and sincere, and people would respond to that at once. She was also very pretty, and that didn't hurt, either.

Then he caught the gist of their conversation, and his heart stopped.

"Well, Adam gave the impression that he wasn't very interested in reading these days." Marina said, sounding wistful.

Mrs Brown sighed. "His father – the old Duke, that is – didn't encourage reading. He considered it a real waste of time. He never bothered with reading. If I'd been caught with a book in my hands, I'd have been dismissed at once. He couldn't stop the servants from reading books in the privacy of their own rooms, of course, but it was greatly discouraged, and forbidden in the servants' halls. Oh, and we weren't allowed to take books from the library."

"Really? But you said that he rarely read them himself."

Mrs Brown snorted. "No, he didn't. These books mostly went untouched until his Grace became the Duke. Now, we can borrow books whenever we like. We sign them in and out, from a ledger by the door, so that all the books can be kept track of, but that's not a hardship."

"That is surprising." Marina murmured, eyeing the book in her hands. It was Mysteries of Udolpho, Adam noted.

He was vaguely aware that he shouldn't be eavesdropping on a private conversation, but this was his house, after all.

"He's a good man, your Grace." Mrs Brown said, her voice carefully light and neutral. "It's not my place to say, of course, but he does seem to struggle with showing his feelings. Again, that was the old Duke. I remember once his Grace stood between me and his father, pretending to lean against one of the bookshelves, so that I could put a book back before the old Duke could see me reading it." Mrs Brown paused, chuckling. "I was foolish, of course. I was a grown woman, and he was just a child. He reminded me of a younger brother I had, who died quite young. But his Grace was always exceptionally kind to everyone."

Adam sucked in a breath. He remembered that moment. He'd been scolded for his father for wasting so much time in the library.

Then he glanced up and caught Marina looking straight at him through the open door.

"Adam, there you are!" Marina exclaimed. "I didn't see you at breakfast."

There was nothing for it but to smile and step inside. Adam glanced at Mrs Brown, to see if she felt guilty over revealing such a private moment to Marina, but the wretched housekeeper was simply smiling cheerfully.

"Yes, I had rather a lot of work to do." Adam said, aware that his voice sounded clipped and brusque.

He wished Mrs Brown wouldn't talk to Marina about his childhood. He already regretted saying what he did about the library. It was much better to keep their respective personal lives wholly separate.

Marina didn't care about his personal life. She didn't care about the Adam that skulked in the library, devouring books until he realized that it made his father angry. She didn't want to hear how Adam covered up for a servant who was reading when she ought to be cleaning.

There was no way she would want to hear any of that.

But when Adam raised his eyes, he found Marina was watching him again, a soft smile playing about her lips.

There was something about that tiny, almost-smile that made his breath hitch in his throat. He swallowed hard, squeezing his hands into fists to get a hold of himself again.

"I'm glad that you've discovered the library, Marina." He said shortly. "I'm sure you'll enjoy the books. Do help yourself to whatever you like. Since this belongs to you now, I suppose you don't need to worry about signing out the books."

Marina gave a short laugh. "Oh, I don't mind. Rules are for everyone, aren't they?"

"Will you be requiring use of the library, your Grace?" Mrs Brown inquired. "As per your requirements, some of the older and rarer books have been locked away. Do let me know if you want them taken out again. If you like, we could even…"

"No, thank you." Adam said, cutting her off. He internally winced at his rudeness, but the air in the library was becoming hot and stifling in a way that it never had before. He suddenly wanted to leave, more than anything else in the world, and began to back towards the door.

Marina was watching him again, nibbling on her lower lip.

"Are you alright, Adam?" she asked, her voice soft. "You seem upset."

"I'm quite alright." He snapped, and Marina recoiled a little.

"What I meant was that I am busy." Adam amended, flushing. "I don't have time to waste on things as pointless and frivolous as reading. You can do as you like, of course, but if you'll excuse me, I have real work to do."

Adam turned on his heel, marching out of the library. He pulled the door closed behind him. Neither Mrs Brown nor Marina had responded to his outburst, not that he'd given them a chance to do so.

Shame washed over Adam like a bucket of cold water. He wished that he hadn't been so short with them. He forced himself to keep going, to keep striding down the hallway towards the staircase.

You don't have time for this, he reminded himself. Besides, do you really want to spend hours in the library with Marina? Does that seem like a good idea to you?

No, it did not. Theirs was, as he was continually reminding himself, a marriage of convenience, and it wasn't fair at all to think of Marina in another other way beyond cool, disinterested friendship.

Chapter Twenty-One

There was an awkward silence in the library after Adam left. Marina couldn't quite meet Mrs Brown's eyes.

"I... I'm sorry about that." Marina said, not entirely sure why she had to apologise at all for Adam's behaviour. "I suppose I should have worded that more carefully."

Mrs Brown bit her lip and shook her head. "You have nothing to apologise for, my dear. I'm only sorry that your new husband is too busy with business to attend to you. That must be difficult."

Marina gave a short laugh. "Ah, I see you don't know."

Mrs Brown raised an eyebrow. "Don't know what?"

"Our marriage is one of convenience. It was arranged quite coolly, and there any many benefits on both sides."

"Ah. Well, I can't say I'm surprised – his Grace always preferred to do things calmly and in a well-arranged manner. I always hoped to see him fall in love first. Still, there is time for that."

It took Marina an embarrassing half-minute to realise that Mrs Brown was referring to him falling in love with her, his wife. She flushed and laughed uncomfortably.

"Oh, I'm sure that won't happen. We're both very pleased with the way things have turned out. I'm a duchess, after all."

Marina immediately wished that she hadn't said that. It sounded as if being a duchess was all she cared about.

But Mrs Brown didn't seem shocked or annoyed. She only eyed Marina with a strange expression for a moment or two, then nodded, smiling.

"As long as you're both happy, that is all that matters."

She turned away, rearranging some books on the bookshelf. Marina
hesitated, working up the courage to ask her next question.

The truth was, it was nearly impossible to reconcile the young boy of Mrs Brown's stories – the boy who loved books and wanted to help others – with the grown man that Marina knew, who was cold and sharp and brusque.

What had changed? What happened?

"What was Adam like when you knew him?" Marina burst out. "I mean... do you think he's changed? What do you think of him now?"

Mrs Brown hesitated, flashing a guarded look at her.

"He is my employer, your Grace. He's a good man, and I'm fond of him."

Marina flushed. "I didn't mean... that is, I know he's a good man, but he seems different now to the way you described him. If I didn't know better, I'd say that you were describing two different people."

Mrs Brown paused, fingers skimming over the spines of the books. She was thinking, nibbling on her lower lip, weighing up the risks.

Marina waited, holding her breath.

"I'm not sure what you want me to tell you, your Grace." She said, voice light and conversational. "Of course, I want to help, but discretion is a valued quality in a housekeeper."

Marina let out the breath she'd been holding.

"I'm not mining for gossip. Truly, I'm not. I just... well, I've married this man. Sometimes I feel so drawn to Adam, and other times, it's as if he'd push me away, holding me at arm's length. It's confusing. I'd just like to get to know him a little bit better, that's all."

She waited again, forcing herself to be patient. If Mrs Brown chose not to speak to her about Adam, Marina wasn't sure what she would do. She could probably insist, as the Duchess of Brixham, but that was hardly a good start.

Mrs Brown sighed, turning back from the bookshelves.

"Alright, your Grace. I'll tell you as much as I can, assuming that it will stay between us."

Marina resisted the urge to grin in relief.

"Thank you, I appreciate that."

"What would you like to know?"

"Tell me about the old Duke." Marina said. She wasn't sure where that question had come from, but somehow that was the first one to spring to her mind.

Mrs Brown's expression hardened.

"He was not a good man. I don't wish to speak ill of the dead, and his Grace was very devoted to his father. But the old Duke of Brixham was not a pleasant man, not at all. He neglected his wife, abused all the servants, and wrung every penny out of his tenants that he could. He was a deeply unfeeling man and had a warped view of what a man and a duke ought to be. As a young boy, his Grace was a very sensitive child, and the old Duke did not like that. Not one bit. He decided to wring out every drop of kindness and pity from his son, and some days I fear that he succeeded."

That sent a chill down Marina's spine.

"Was he really so cruel?"

Mrs Brown nodded. "I'm afraid so. Ask the tenants about him, or some of the older servants, if you're feeling brave. We were all afraid of the old Duke, and for good reason. His moods were always changing, and you could never tell when he would suddenly turn on you. This house was a different place when he was alive."

"Goodness, that's awful." Marina absorbed this, biting her lip. "But Adam was fond of him?"

"Oh, yes. Boys are usually fond of their fathers. His Grace was keen to please his father, and determined to live up to the standard of what he perceived as perfection. He adored his father, and it was painful to watch at times. The old Duke's criticism cut deep, and he never praised him. I often wonder what damage that sort of childhood might have on a person."

Mrs Brown sighed, shaking her head. She had a distant, wistful expression on her face, as if lost in some memory playing in her mind. Marina almost felt as though she were intruding on a private moment. She was just wondering whether it would be polite to sneak away and leave Mrs Brown to her thoughts when the woman gave a little shake of her head, straightened up, and smiled.

"I beg your pardon; I was a million miles away. Was there anything else you wanted to know?"

"Yes, actually. When did Adam start to change? I mean, if he was a sweet boy at one time, when did he start to become more like..."

She trailed off, but Mrs Brown finished the sentence for her.

"More like his father?" she said archly. "It began when he was thirteen years old. Until then, his Grace was able to do more or less what he liked. The Duke didn't seem particularly interested in him, although of course his Grace adored his father. Then, when he turned thirteen, the old Duke decided that now was the time to start teaching his son about how to be a duke, and how the world worked. Or at least, his idea of how the world worked, and what a duke and a man ought to be." She bit her lip, shaking her head again. "We all saw it happening. It was awful, watching a sweet, loving little boy become something cold and heartless. The old Duke was thrilled, of course. That was exactly what he wanted. Even the Duchess – that is, the Dowager Duchess – wasn't able to do anything about it."

"Goodness." Marina managed.

She was quiet for a moment or two, thinking. It was a bleak picture – an earnest young boy who adored his father, slowly but surely being remade into someone harsh, cold, and unkind. Was that sort of change irreversible? Marina was afraid that it might be.

One thing was sure, though. Adam would not be happy to know that she'd had this discussion with Mrs Brown.

She eyed the housekeeper and smiled uncertainly.

"Thank you for your honesty. I appreciate it. Perhaps it might be best if you don't mention to Adam that I've spoken to you about this."

Mrs Brown chuckled. "Oh, you needn't worry about that. I certainly won't."

Chapter Twenty-Two

"And you say that Elias has moved back your boundary line a full foot?" Adam said, glancing down at a document before him.

The man before him, Thomas, was a tenant, and had chosen this time to bring up a dispute with his neighbour.

The hours had flown by, as they tended to do when you were busy. Adam had met tenant after tenant, trying desperately to retain their names. Matthew followed him around the villages, carrying a heavy, open ledger detailing how much every tenant 'owed', and how they could alleviate the debt.

It was exhausting, but Adam found that he liked the way his tenants' faces lit up in relief when he explained that a mistake had been made, and that they did not have to repay the money that had been stolen.

"Thomas, Elias, we will discuss this later." Matthew spoke up, his voice soft but carrying undeniable authority. Apparently, he was well-known in the community, and respected, too.

It was hard not to admire that.

The two men backed away, making stiff bows and glaring at each other out of the corners of their eyes.

Matthew closed the ledger with a snap.

"I thought you might like to return for luncheon, your Grace." He said, glancing up at the sun.

Adam followed his gaze and was surprised at much time had gone by.

"Yes, of course. Thank you for your help, Matthew."

Matthew blinked, taken aback at the compliment.

"I appreciate that, your Grace. I believe that our meeting today has been very productive. Shall we resume work after luncheon?"

"Yes, that sounds like it would be best."

The two men strode out of the village, with Adam waving goodbye to the villagers who waved at him.

Their horses were tied up just at the edge of the village, with plenty of grass and a full horse trough of water available. Adam's mind was working twenty to the dozen as he climbed up into the saddle.

It wasn't just the business with the tenants and their rents that was bothering Adam.

"My father had a very straightforward opinion on apologies." Adam said suddenly.

Matthew, half poised to climb into his own saddle, paused and glanced over his shoulder.

"I beg your pardon, your Grace?"

Adam pursed his lips. "Do you think a duke ought ever to apologise? My father thought not."

Matthew hauled himself into the saddle and settled himself comfortably.

"I am aware of what the old Duke believed." Matthew replied shortly. "Personally, I believe a man should apologise when it is required. Regardless of his birth or station."

Adam considered this. It was hardly a ground-breaking opinion, but the old Duke believed that noble men were rarely in the wrong, if ever, and if they were, somebody else should absorb the blame. That would leave the noble man free to remain on his lofty pedestal for as long as he wanted, unhindered by such mundane things as making mistakes.

He glanced at Matthew, feeling a newfound respect for the man. He and Matthew were too different to be friends, and he was well aware that Matthew did not particularly like him. Still, he'd seen how the villagers responded to Matthew, and they seemed fond of him.

That had to count for something, surely?

"I think you are right." Adam said. "I'm glad you suggested a break for luncheon, because I have an apology to make. Two, in fact."

Matthew eyed him curiously, then inclined his head gracefully.

"Very good, your Grace."

The apologies, of course, were to Mrs Brown and Marina.

Adam's own sharp words had lingered in his mind for hours, quietly reproaching him. He shouldn't have been so unkind to them. He would have made Mrs Brown feel small and out of place, and Marina was already having to adjust to a completely new sort of life with a stranger.

Adam should not have made her feel so uncomfortable, especially over something like books and reading.

It wasn't her fault he didn't have time for his own hobbies these days.

Adam and Matthew parted ways at the edge of the hall's grounds. Adam dismounted near the stables, handing over his horse to a groom. He smoothed his palms down his clothes – unfashionable, practical, and a little grubby – and drew in a deep breath.

It was a fine day. The sun was shining, the sky was blue, and birds twittered idyllically in the treetops.

Adam paused for a moment, glancing around the well-manicured gardens. His gardens. It was still strange, all these years later, to think that these gardens, the house, and everything all belonged to him. Part of Adam still expected to glance up at the house and see the old Duke lingering in a window, frowning down at him in displeasure over some mistake or misdemeanour.

Whenever he opened the study door, he held his breath, expecting to see his father sitting in state behind the desk, papers neatly arranged before him, craggy eyebrows drawn low over his eyes.

Adam closed his eyes, remembering how he would fidget for minutes on end before his father's desk, listening to the scratch-scratch of a pen nib on paper, waiting for his father to look up and notice him.

It had been a power play, of course, although it had taken Adam an embarrassingly long time to work that out. The old Duke took pleasure in summoning people to his study only to keep them waiting, fidgeting without a chair, while he scribbled diligently away at some task that could certainly wait until after his meeting.

It was an unkind thing to do, and Adam had been careful not to do that himself.

He opened his eyes, squinting in the bright sunlight, and decided that he wouldn't think about that anymore. This was his house, and he had to come to terms with that sooner or later.

After all, he'd brought his own duchess here, which a clear way of staking his claim.

Adam's stomach, still mourning the loss of breakfast, grumbled, reminding him why he'd returned.

He began to stride through the maze of well-groomed hedges and flowerbeds. His footsteps crunched on the gravel, which had been raked only that morning. Some of Adam's worries began to melt away, in the way that only a sunny day and a good mood can achieve.

Then he heard a low chuckle from his left and paused.

Towards the west wing of the house, the low hedges and neat flowerbeds gave way to riotous undergrowth, tree glades, and cultivated wilderness. He could see a small clearing amongst the trees, carpeted with moss. This clearing was unique, as wild roses grew all around it, colourful and sweet-smelling. A small bench had been placed there, and a young woman curled up on the bench, chuckling at something she was reading in a book.

It was Marina, of course.

Adam watched her, engrossed in her book, and felt his heart began to pound, leaving him breathless.

She was unaware of his presence, and Adam knew that he ought to do something to draw attention to himself. He should cough, or call out to her, or just walk away and leave the poor woman alone to read her book.

He did none of those things. Instead, Adam began to walk closer, drawn by something he didn't quite understand.

Chapter Twenty-Three

Mysteries of Udolpho was extremely funny, although Marina had the impression that it wasn't meant to be funny.

She chuckled at a particular passage, shaking her head. The heroine was likeable, but in a frail, silly sort of way. Marina herself had never swooned, and her friends rarely swooned, too. Emily St Aubert, however, seemed to swoon at the drop of a hat. It was annoying when she fainted at a crucial moment in the story, leaving the reader to wait impatiently for her to wake up again, so that the story could resume.

A crunch of gravel made Marina jump, glancing up sharply.

Adam was there, only ten feet away, and she started in earnest.

The book slipped form her hands, landing face-down on the gravel.

Marina scrambled to her feet, cheeks red.

How long had he been watching her?

"Your Grace. Adam." She said, dropping a quick curtsey.

Adam shook his head, bending to pick up the book.

"I think you can dispense with the curtsies, just as we dispensed with the 'your graces'. I was looking for you, in fact. You've chosen a pretty place to read."

Marina watched him brush gravel off the book's cover, tenderly straightening out the crumpled pages.

"Thank you." she managed. "I didn't see you at breakfast."

Adam didn't meet her eye. "I had a great deal of work to do. And I wasn't hungry."

As if to prove him wrong, Adam's stomach grumbled loudly. A flush of colour rose to his cheeks, and Marina fought back a smile.

"I see." She said innocently. "Will you be joining us for luncheon, then?"

"Us?"

"Me." She amended. "Or will I be able to read my book at the dining table again?"

Adam smiled at that. "You're the Duchess of Brixham. You can do what you like."

Marina had to smile back. "Yes, I keep forgetting that. It's very exciting."

He was still holding the book in his hands, his gaze fixed on the cover. Marina itched to reach out and take it back – she hadn't marked her place – and folded her hands in front of her to fight back the urge.

"I owe you an apology." Adam blurted out.

Marina blinked. She hadn't been expecting that.

"I... I beg your pardon?"

He drew in a deep breath, looking up to meet her gaze.

There was something about his steady, clear gaze that made Marina shiver. In a good way, that is.

If one could shiver in a good way.

"I was extremely rude to both you and Mrs Brown in the library earlier. You were only trying to be kind, and I was sharp and unkind. I'm on my way to apologise to Mrs Brown, but I'll take this opportunity to offer my apologies to you now. I shouldn't have spoken to you like that. What I said was true – I often don't have time for reading – but I was also disparaging of reading as a hobby. That's not my real opinion. I daresay I was defensive, and you and Mrs Brown shouldn't have had to deal with that."

He took a breath, seeming to deflate a little. Marina eyed him, wondering how long he'd been planning that apology. He was waiting for her to respond, still holding the book in his hands.

He seemed... expectant. Hopeful. Nervous.

No, not nervous. Adam Blackburn, the formidable Duke of Brixham, couldn't possibly be nervous.

Marina reached out for the book, and Adam blinked, seeming to wake up. He handed the book to her – keeping his finger in the pages to mark her place, she noticed with relief – and Marina accepted it.

Their fingers brushed when she took the book. It was an accident of course, but the touch sent tingles across Marina's skin. His fingers were warm and dry, familiar and yet entirely unfamiliar.

She sucked in a breath, masking her confusion by hugging the book to her chest.

"Please, think no more of it." Marina said. "We all speak out of turn at times. I daresay Mrs Brown and I ought not to have nagged you to spend time reading. I know you're busy, and I know that you came here to work."

Adam nodded, seeming... what? Relieved? Nervous?

"You're very kind, thank you."

Marina waited for him to turn and leave, but he was just standing there. Without the book in his hands, Adam began to pick at his fingers, glancing around.

What does he want from me? Marina thought. And why don't I want him to go?

Once she'd conjured up the thought, Marina realized in shock that it was true. She didn't want him to go.

She glanced around, trying to think of something to say. After all, she ought to put him at his ease now that he'd been man enough to apologise.

That was the only reason.

"The roses are very beautiful." Marina burst out. "I like wild roses better than cultivated ones. Not that the rose gardens aren't pretty." She added hastily, in case he thought that she was being critical.

Adam smiled. "Yes, they're beautiful. My mother planted them, in fact. She liked a little chaos in her garden. She said that the manicured hedges and immaculate flowerbeds felt wrong. Nature is untidy, that's what she'd say." He chuckled to himself, shaking his head.

"Nature is untidy." Marina echoed, smiling. "I like that. I'm surprised that she hasn't changed the gardens more, then."

Adam shrugged, smile fading. "Father would never allow her. I suppose she just got tired of fighting with him. I would let her make whatever changes she wanted, of course, but I think Mother is past the age when she wants to make changes. She would always say that once I got married, I would have a duchess who would want to make her own mark."

Marina considered this, tilting her head to one side.

"I might ask Evelyn if she wanted to help me make some improvements to the gardens, then. There's not a leaf out of place on those hedges. It must take a lot of work, but it doesn't feel right, does it?"

Adam's smile began to return. He had a strange expression on his face, one that made Marina's heart flutter in a way she could not control.

"I think Mother would like that. She already thinks you're the perfect daughter-in-law."

Marina snorted. "She doesn't know me very well, then."

Adam held her gaze for a long moment. The air in the clearing seemed to get heavier, the sweet smell of roses becoming more overpowering by the instant.

Adam looked away first, and Marina let out a breath she hadn't even realized that she was holding. He stepped to the side of the clearing, leaning over a spray of white roses, their centres a rich, dappled yellow.

He withdrew a small pocketknife from his pocket, and neatly snipped off one perfect bloom at the stem.

Marina watched, mesmerized. He held the rose for an instant, looking down at it with an unreadable expression on his face.

Then he turned to her and held out the flower.

"For you." Adam said, his voice quiet. "I'll let you get on with your reading now. Good day, Marina."

Marina took the rose, an automatic reaction more than anything else, finding herself unable to look away from Adam's steady, intent gaze.

"Thank you." she said, breathless.

He gave a short, graceless bow, then turned and walked away. Marina watched him go, fingers wrapped around the rose's stem, not quite able to absorb what had just happened.

Who are you? Marina thought, bewildered. And what have you done with the real Adam Blackburn?

Chapter Twenty-Four

The walk from the pretty little glade to the house took around ten minutes. That gave Adam a full ten minutes to contemplate how much of a fool he'd been. What had he been thinking, offering Marina a rose like that?

It was the sort of gesture that couldn't be misinterpreted. It was romantic — or hopefully romantic, at least — and she couldn't possibly have misread it.

He clenched his teeth, resisting the urge to groan aloud. How could he have been so stupid?

He tried to conjure up an image of what Marina's expression had been like when he handed her the rose.

Surprised, certainly. Baffled, perhaps.

Was she laughing at him? Did she toss the rose away as soon as his back was turned, and resume reading her book with a sigh?

Adam couldn't imagine Marina doing something so cruel. He'd only known her for a little while, and already he knew that she was a kind, empathetic young woman.

Perhaps she'd just feel sorry for him.

Adam's face burned. It was a relief to step out of the bright sunlight of the garden into the cool of the hallway.

He stood for a moment, breathing in deeply and closing his eyes.

"Your Grace?"

Julian's voice made him jump.

"Sorry, Julian, I was miles away. What is it?"

Adam opened his eyes and forced a smile. Julian was the youngest butler Adam had ever met by miles — the man was barely thirty. Still, he was efficient, and very well-liked by the servants. Since Adam spent so much time away from his country-seat, it was important that his household could rub along together well enough without his being there.

Julian was Mrs Brown's nephew, which was in part why he'd originally been hired as a footman. He had the same kindly, intent expression on his face that Adam often saw on Mrs Brown's.

The guilt over snapping at his old friend increased. He had no doubt that Mrs Brown wouldn't have told Julian about it, but that wasn't the point.

"Where is Mrs Brown, Julian?"

"In the kitchen, I believe." Julian replied. "Shall I fetch her for you, your Grace?"

"No, I'll find her myself. If you do run into her, let her know that I'm looking for her. I was rather sharp with her last night, and I need to offer an apology."

Julian nodded and turned to leave.

"Oh, and one last thing, Julian."

The butler turned back, one eyebrow raised.

Adam closed his eyes. The sting of mortification hadn't quite faded over that business with Marina and the rose. He was about to take the coward's way out, but this was his home and he could be as cowardly as he liked.

Perhaps he'd used up all of his goodwill on meeting his tenants that morning.

"I won't be eating in the dining room at dinner tonight. I'll take a tray in my study, if you don't mind."

Julian's expression did not change, but he would know that Marina was eating in the dining room. He would know that Adam had just condemned her to eat alone. Again.

"Very good, your Grace." Julian said neutrally.

***

Marina twirled the rose in her fingers, breathing in the scent of the bloom.

It really was a perfect rose. A little tingle ran through her whenever she remembered how Adam had looked when he handed it to her. The moment replayed over and over in her head.

She wished she'd said something more meaningful or looked a little less shocked and a little more happy. It had just been such a surprise. Adam had never seemed to be the sort of person who offered flowers.

"That's a pretty bloom, your Grace." Geraldine said, passing behind Marina with a pile of neatly folded linens. "Shall I fetch a vase and some water? You could put it on your nightstand."

"Thank you, Geraldine, I will." Marina hesitated for a moment. "His Grace gave it to me."

She had no one else to talk to about this subject, and Geraldine seemed as good a confidante as any.

Geraldine paused, eyes lighting up.

"What a kind gesture, your Grace. Did he pick it especially for you?"

Marina smiled to herself, stroking the soft petals. "Yes, he did. I was surprised. His Grace often seems... well, distant, I suppose. I was under no illusions about that when we married..." she paused and cleared her throat, awkwardly aware that she really shouldn't be talking to Geraldine about this. "Anyway. It was a surprise, and a pleasant one."

Geraldine began putting the linens away, chewing her lower lip thoughtfully.

"His Grace seems very fond of you." she said finally. "I know it's not my place, but I do know that many newly married couples have a sort of... sort of awkwardness between them. Perhaps it will take you and his Grace a little time to grow accustomed to each other."

Marina considered this. She did feel as if she were growing accustomed to Adam. She looked forward to his presence more than she'd dreaded it, and the vast, sprawling house was starting to feel like theirs, rather than just his.

"I think you're right." she said. "So, what should I do next? I feel like we're becoming friends, and I'd like us to be friends. I'd like that very much."

Geraldine's face lit up.

"I know exactly what we can do, your Grace."

Marina met Geraldine's eye through the dresser mirror.

"Well, I'm listening."

***

Marina paused on the landing, not entirely sure why she

suddenly felt so nervous.

Geraldine had picked out a delicate pink gown, a simpler design than the vibrant emerald one, with embroidered white flowers on the hem, bodice, and sleeves.

She'd done up Marina's hair in a simpler style than before too, one that felt more comfortable – the sort of hairstyle Marina could wear every day, if necessary. Her hair was twisted up towards the back of her head, with ringlets cascading down onto her neck and around her ears. Marina had glanced at herself in the mirror before stepping out of her room and was hugely pleased with the results.

She drew in a breath. If she lingered on the landing any longer, she would be late for dinner. She descended, twirling the white rose between her fingers. It seemed silly to bring it along with her, but the flower almost felt like a talisman.

She stepped into the hallway, her footsteps echoing in the quiet. The dining room door was open, and the room beyond was full of light and warmth. The long table was laden with food, but Adam was not there.

Marina stood, frowning. It wasn't like him to be late.

Then she noticed that the table was only set with one place.

A nasty, cold feeling tingled down Marina's spine. She turned to Julian, who had that butler-y trick of being exactly where you wanted him at the moment that you wanted.

"Julian, where is his Grace?"

Something passed over Julian's face that might well have been pity.

"His Grace is taking a tray in his study." Julian replied, his voice betraying no emotion at all.

Marina flinched. "Oh. I... I didn't know that."

"Are you quite well, your Grace? A tray can be sent to your room or to one of the parlours, if you would prefer to eat there."

She drew in a breath. "No, thank you. The food is all set out here. Thank you, Julian."

He bowed and moved back.

Marina settled herself in the place set for her at the head of the table. A sharp pain ran through her finger, and she realized that she'd pricked herself on one of the rose's thorns.

How apt, Marina thought bitterly, tossing the flower onto the table. That's what will happen to me if I let myself develop feelings for this man. I shall get hurt.

Chapter Twenty-Five

Adam dreamt about his childhood. As dreams of that sort often go, it was not a pleasant one.

When the curtains were pulled open and light flooded into the room, Adam squinted against the light, feeling as though he hadn't slept at all.

Scenes from his dream last night had been all too common. His father, lip curled and contempt on his face, speaking harshly to Evelyn over the dinner table. He remembered how Evelyn used to shrink in her seat, colour rushing to her face.

By the time Adam was old enough to realize that the way his father treated Evelyn was wrong, he already loved his father too much to hate him for it. So, Adam tried to balance his feelings for his father and his feelings for his mother.

It had never been easy. Now that the old Duke was gone, it was harder than ever.

Adam rolled onto his back and sighed. He was vaguely aware of his valet hovering politely in the corner of the room, waiting for Adam to get up so he could help him get dressed.

"Is her Grace up?" Adam heard himself say.

Why had he chosen to ask that?

"I believe she is awake but has not yet left her rooms. I understand that her Grace plans to go down to breakfast shortly."

Adam closed his eyes. If last night's dream was anything to go by, his subconscious mind was telling him to treat Marina better. His own conscience was telling him the same.

"How quickly can you help me get ready, then?"

The plush carpet absorbed the sound of Adam's footsteps. He hurried along the curving hallway towards the landing. Marina might already be down at breakfast, and he might not get a chance to speak to her again.

I hope you aren't going to apologise, boy, said a severe voice in the back of Adam's head, which sounded too much like his father. *Noblemen have no need to apologise. Dukes don't make mistakes, and therefore have no reason to apologise.*

He walked a little faster, straining his ears to see if he could hear any clinking of cutlery from the dining room. He rounded the corner and burst out onto the landing, at the exact same moment that Marina went hurtling into him.

She knocked into him, hands flying out to steady herself. She would have gone bouncing backwards and probably landed in an unceremonious heap on the landing carpet, if Adam hadn't grabbed her arms.

"Steady on." He said, hardly thinking about it.

Then he realized that Marina's hands were spread out against his chest, the warmth of her palms seeming to sink through the material onto his skin.

His breath skipped in his throat.

They were only inches apart, with the top of Marina's head level with Adam's chin. She looked up at the same moment that he looked down, and he could have sworn that all of the air was stolen from the room.

"I beg your pardon." Marina said, her voice tight.

She stepped back, slipping her upper arms out of Adam's grasp. Her hands moved from his chest, and he missed their warmth. Marina dropped her hands back down to her side, clutching at her skirts.

"It was an accident." Adam said, clearing his throat. "I should have been watching where I was going."

She bit her lip, glancing away. Adam inspected her face, disturbed to find that she was pale, her eyes ringed with dark circles.

"Have you been sleeping, Marina?"

He wasn't sure where that had come from. Marina flinched, glancing up at him with a frown.

"Yes, thank you. Have you been sleeping?"

That last question sounded almost like a challenge. Adam wanted to smile, but reminded himself that Marina was clearly not happy with him at the moment.

No prizes for guessing why not.

"I have, thank you."

"Good." Marina turned towards the stairs, and Adam realized with a spurt of panic that his chance to talk this over was quickly running out.

"Marina, wait. Please."

She paused, hand hovering over the banister.

"What is it, Adam? I know how busy you are."

He winced. Now that was pointed.

"I owe you an apology."

She narrowed her eyes. "You apologised yesterday, didn't you? Or have you forgotten already?"

There was a definite tinge of bitterness in her voice. Adam swallowed hard.

"I didn't attend dinner last night. I heard from Julian that you did."

"What did you expect me to do, Adam?"

He shook his head, taking a hesitant step forward.

"I am too used to only thinking about myself, Marina. I was brought up that way. It's no excuse, I know, but I ought to be more fair towards you. The least I can do is spend our mealtimes together – if you want that, of course."

She eyed him for a long moment, considering. It occurred to Adam that perhaps she would prefer him to eat his meals alone. Perhaps he'd already pushed her too far, and Marina had lost whatever passing interest she had in him at the start.

He was shocked at how miserable that thought made him feel. It was a physical thing, an ache in his chest like a stab of indigestion.

It was strange how many emotions felt like indigestion. The resemblance was uncanny, in Adam's opinion.

Marina sighed, waking him out of his contemplation of the connection between strong emotion and indigestion.

"Let's have breakfast, then."

She tilted her head to one side, holding out her hand. It was a gesture, one that Adam hadn't expected to encounter.

He reached out in turn, taking her hand in his. Her hand was small and soft, and seemed to fit inside his larger one absolutely perfectly.

A soft smile spread out over Marina's face. Her eyes were still fixed on him, and Adam felt as though he could not physically tear his gaze away.

"Come on, then. I'm starving." She said, laughing, and the spell was broken.

For a good while, there was only the sounds of clinking cutlery and polite chewing.

The servants had apparently not expected Adam to come down for breakfast – they could hardly be blamed, since he'd missed breakfast for at least the last two days, not to mention taking a tray in his rooms at every opportunity – and there was something of a fluster when the two of them walked in together.

As a result, Marina and Adam were seated at opposite ends of the table, too far apart to comfortably conduct a conversation.

Not that Adam could think of anything to say.

Come on, man, he scolded himself. You're an interesting person, are you not? Start a conversation. Just pick a topic!

It was no use. His mind was going blank, as if he'd never held an interest, engaged in a hobby, or conducted a conversation in his life.

It would be funny if it wasn't so infuriating.

In the end, they both spoke at the same time.

"So how is your book..."

"Are you going out to the..."

Awkward silence fell.

"You go first."

"No, you."

"Ladies first."

"Your conversation sounded more interesting."

"Very well." Adam cleared his throat, setting down his knife and fork. "Are you enjoying your book?"

She smiled. "Very much so."

"I'm glad to hear it. What were you going to say?"

Marina kept her eyes on her plate. "Are you going out to work today?"

Adam swallowed. "Yes, I'm afraid I must. You... you don't mind, do you?"

"Mind? Of course not." Marina glanced up, meeting his eye and placing a forkful of bacon in her mouth. "That's what we're here for, after all, isn't it? Work. Yours, to be precise."

Adam cleared his throat again, feeling as though he'd missed a beat somewhere along the line.

Chapter Twenty-Six

Two Days Later

Marina was bored.

At home, she'd never have confessed to something so shocking.

"Bored people are boring." Letitia would say severely, before assigning some awful chore for Marina to complete.

She'd learned to entertain herself at an early age. When they fell on hard times, there was always some chore to be done, some task to be completed that the servants couldn't manage, and those chores filled up most of Marina's time.

Brixham Hall was entirely different. There was nothing for Marina to do, except for wandering around the house and reading books. She'd spent hours reading, but even that got tiring after a while. Besides, hunching over a book for hours on end couldn't possibly be good for her posture. She had no friends in this area, nobody to visit, and she'd already drafted out letters for just about everybody she could think of, back home in London. She hadn't received any letters back yet, which was a pity.

And now she was well and truly bored. The promised tour from Mrs Brown hadn't taken place, and Marina didn't want to nag the poor woman. No doubt she had better things to do than to show a bored duchess around her new home.

And so Marina was left to wander alone.

She was conducting an exploration of the second floor when she turned a corner and spotted a door she hadn't noticed before.

The door was painted a pale pink, so it was something she would have noticed before.

Marina hesitated, fingers inches away from the handle.

Should she go in?

This is your house too, Marina reminded herself fiercely. This isn't Adam's rooms, or his study, so why shouldn't you be able to go inside?

Thus decided, she turned the doorknob and stepped inside.

The room appeared to be another parlour, or perhaps a little morning-room. It was certainly catching plenty of sunlight and afforded beautiful views of the grounds.

The room was a little too comfortable to be a fashionable parlour, and of course it wasn't ideal to usher visitors upstairs in any case. No, this little space seemed like somebody's personal room.

Surprisingly, the room was decorated entirely in shades of pink, ranging from the palest pink – almost white – to a shade of vibrant cerise. It reminded Marina of her purple-hued bedroom back home. Just like her room, the shades of colour were well-chosen, not overwhelming. In fact, the room almost had a gentle, soothing ambience to it.

There were sofas, well-worn and comfortable, and a little circular coffee table in the middle. The coffee table was a little chipped and marked, but seemed well-loved, nonetheless. From the windows – hung with white-pink lace curtains – Marina spotted the tree-glade where she'd sat before, when Adam had given her that rose. She stood there for a long moment, looking down into the garden.

She could see gardeners and various servants moving here and there, talking to each other and getting on with work. It felt as if Marina was looking in on something that didn't concern her, so she let the curtain fall back, and turned back towards the pink room. There was more to be seen here. She might find herself sitting up here alone for years to come, while Adam went about his life, pretending he didn't have a wife at all.

She shook off that thought. It had been two days since he had apologised for leaving her to eat dinner alone. They'd had breakfast together, and once again, Marina had thought that she and Adam might have turned a corner after all.

Ha. How wrong she was.

Adam had more or less avoided her entirely over the past two days. He'd attended dinner with her, but that was all. They didn't even talk much. Hope was quickly ebbing away, and Marina was starting to feel truly miserable.

She wished they could just get back to London and get on with their separate lives.

To distract herself, Marina paced around the little pink room. It was full of trinkets and knickknacks. There was a little silver jewellery box, elaborately carved, perched on a shelf. A small bookshelf was stacked full of books – novels, all well-read and dog-eared.

Evelyn liked novels, didn't she? Marina wondered whether this had been her room, when she was the Duchess of Brixham.

She ran her finger along the books' spines, lost in thought.

How many hours had Evelyn spent up here? Had she wept tears for her unfeeling husband and her son, who was quickly going the way of his father?

Marina swallowed hard, turning away.

There were a series of small, thin-legged table perched along the wall, each bearing antique vases and delicate ornaments. There seemed to be no order to the trinkets and antiques. They were just precious things, memorable to somebody.

Marina paused before a bowl-shaped vase, swelling up and out from a narrow base. It seemed precariously large for the small table it rested upon. She longed to touch the intricately carved flowers rioting along the side of the vase but decided against it.

These things looked valuable. Judging from the faint sheen of dust over everything, Marina guessed that this room was rarely used, and that the maids were nervous about dusting things that were so valuable.

She didn't blame them.

Then the door flew open with a bang, and Marina spun around with a shriek.

Her skirt caught the delicate little table, dragging it away from the wall and upending it with a crash.

The vase on top went spinning into the air, shattering on the smooth wood floor with an almighty smash, shards of porcelain flying everywhere.

Marina slapped her hands against her mouth, eyes wide.

She glanced back to the door to see who'd startled her.

It was Adam. Of course it was Adam. He stood frozen in the doorway, his face an almost comical expression of shock.

"I... I didn't know you were so close to the door." He managed.

Marina couldn't think of anything to say – aside from bellowing a deeply unladylike curse at him – so she turned her attention to the vase.

Her heart sank.

It was, of course, ruined. The vase was now smashed into a thousand pieces, scattered all over the parlour. She gave a moan.

"Was... was it valuable?"

Adam glanced at the broken vase and winced. "I... I believe so. It belongs – belonged – to my mother."

Wonderful. Just wonderful. What would Evelyn think of her now? Not only had Marina taken her place, but now she was breaking her things.

"Perhaps I can fix it." Marina muttered. "If I can just gather up some of the larger pieces..."

She got to her knees beside the majority of the wrecked vase and began gingerly picking up the largest pieces of porcelain.

"Marina, don't. You'll cut yourself."

She shook her head, ignoring him.

Adam gave a tight, angry sigh, and strode over to the bell pull in the corner. He hauled on it twice, then moved over to stand beside Marina.

"Marina..."

"I'm fine." She snapped.

On cue, a particularly sharp piece of porcelain dug itself into her palm. Marina gasped in pain, dropping it automatically.

That was possibly the worst thing she could have done. The razor-sharp piece of pottery sliced open her palm as it fell, and blood welled up.

She bit her lip, hard, and clapped her uninjured hand around her palm. Blood welled up between her fingers.

"Oh, Marina." Adam said.

She went red, feeling ridiculously foolish. "I'm quite alright."

Adam knelt down beside her, pulling out a white handkerchief.

"No." he said, gently but firmly. "You're not."

Chapter Twenty-Seven

Running footsteps sounded down the hall, and Mrs Brown appeared in the doorway, red-faced.

"Oh, your Graces. I was surprised to see the bell ring from the Dowager's old parlour. Is everything alright?"

Her eye fell to Adam's once-white handkerchief, now stained a nasty red, wrapped around her palm.

Mrs Brown turned an unhealthy shade of white.

"Oh, dear. Oh, dear. What happened?"

Marina opened her mouth, not entirely sure how to explain how stupid she'd been.

"A vase fell and broke, and her Grace cut her hand." Adam said shortly. "It's a rather bad cut."

"I... I don't think it's too bad..." Marina began, then got a glimpse of the red gash across her palm. She wasn't usually too worried about the sight of blood, but the redden handkerchief, mingled with the throbbing pain in her palm, made her head swim.

She squeezed her eyes closed, glad of Adam and his handkerchief.

"Marina?"

She opened her eyes to find Adam's face very close to hers, his expression intent and concerned.

"I'm quite alright." Marina said, suddenly afraid that she would do what her favourite heroine Emily St Aubert would do, and faint clean away.

A firm, warm arm wrapped around her shoulders, hugging her close. Marina wanted nothing more than to lean into that embrace and rest her head on Adam's shoulders.

She didn't, of course.

"You aren't alright at all." Adam said, a tinge of worry in his voice. "Mrs Brown, send for Doctor Severn at once, please. With the utmost urgency. Oh, and please have somebody clean up this mess. Carefully, though. I don't want anyone else cutting themselves."

"Of course, your Grace."

Mrs Brown and Adam's voices seemed to be coming from faraway. It was a strange sensation. Marina felt somewhat queasy and didn't dare open her eyes in case she caught a glimpse of her own blood. She could feel it pooling on her palm, hot and sticky, and the pain was getting worse.

Control yourself, she scolded. You're not a simpering heroine. You're going to calm down and handle this small – small! – cut on your hand.

Marina opened her eyes and glanced down at her hand again.

"Oh, dear." She said. "I think I'm going to faint."

***

Marina came round and found herself lying on a couch. Her hand was bandaged, but it still throbbed underneath the layers of linen. She could see a faint red mark in the centre, where her blood must have soaked through.

She glanced around, trying to get her bearings, and realized with a shock that she was in Adam's study.

Adam and Mrs Brown were standing by the door, conversing worriedly.

She cleared her throat, and they both glanced her way.

"Oh, dear." Adam said.

Marina pushed herself into a sitting position, wincing. "Oh, dear? What a welcome."

"It not that." Adam said, moving over to the couch and perching on the edge. "Doctor Severn arrived and inspected your hand while you slept. He says that you'll need stitches, and we'd hoped to do it while you were still unconscious."

"I'll be alright." Marina assured him, with more confidence than she felt. "I'll be fine, truly."

The door opened, and grey-haired, mousy man appeared, clutching a shiny doctor's bag. He smiled weakly at her.

"I see you're awake, Miss, eh…"

"Her Grace the Duchess of Brixham." Adam corrected sharply.

Doctor Severn blushed. "Your Grace, of course. Do forgive me, it's been so long since Brixham Hall had a duchess."

Marina smiled. "Don't worry about it. I keep forgetting that I'm a duchess, too."

Doctor Severn chuckled, the tension in the room broken. He pulled up a chair beside the couch and began unwrapping the bandage on her hand. Marina looked away.

"Did his Grace explain that stitches would be needed?"

"Yes, he did."

"Will you be alright, your Grace?"

Marina drew in a breath and nodded. "Yes, just get it over with quickly. It serves me right for being so silly."

She reached out blindly with her uninjured hand, not quite sure what it was she wanted until she touched it.

She felt her fingers brush the knuckles of Adam's hand and heard him draw in a sharp breath. His hand, balled into a fist, relaxed enough for her to slip her fingers across his palm. Their hands knotted together, and it all seemed to be the most natural thing in the world.

Mrs Brown hovered in the background, looking anxious. She caught
Marina's eye and smiled worriedly. Marina closed her eyes, then just as quickly opened them again, because that seemed to heighten the sensation in her injured hand.

She felt Adam squeeze her uninjured hand, and she glanced at him.

"You'll be alright." He said firmly. "It'll be over before you know it."

Marina drew in a breath and smiled back. It was the strangest thing, but when Adam said things like that, she truly believed him.

Or perhaps she just wanted to believe him.

"This won't take a minute." Doctor Severn said, adjusting his spectacles. "Are you ready?"

***

"That will scar." Marina said, eyeing the red, raised gash across her palm, connected by a series of small, neat, black stitches.

"It'll get infected too, if you keep taking the bandage off."

Adam reprimanded. He picked up the bandages, winding them round and round her hand and carefully knotting the ends together.

True to his word, Doctor Severn had been quick and efficient. The pain hadn't been too bad, and Marina had had Adam's hand in hers to counteract the pain. Mrs Brown was escorting Doctor Severn out, leaving Adam and Marina alone in his study.

Now that it was all over, she felt silly for fainting.

"I don't know what I was thinking." Marina admitted.

Adam shrugged lightly. "I daresay you weren't. It happens sometimes, don't worry about it. You were lucky not to have been more hurt, though. That cut was deep and could have done very serious damage."

Marina nodded, pulling her injured palm into her lap.

"Why did you come bursting in like that, anyway?" she asked. "You almost scared the life out of me."

Adam hesitated.

"I saw you in the window." He admitted, voice soft. A fire had been started in the fireplace, filling the room with light, heat, and the relaxing sound of crackling wood. "I saw you, and I... well, I can't describe it. I had to see you at once. I knew which room you were in. When I was small, Mother used to stand there and wave at me. I shouldn't have barged in like that. It was rude of me."

Marina kept her eyes on Adam's face. His profile was turned to her, and he seemed to be avoiding her eyes. She felt as though she couldn't look away.

"No harm done." she said softly. "At least, there wouldn't have been any harm done if I hadn't gone scrabbling through the broken shards of pottery."

He chuckled at that, raising his eyes to hers.

"I had no idea that you were the sort of person who faints."

"Anyone would have fainted when confronted with such a nasty wound." Marina insisted, but a smile was spreading across her face.

Adam was looking at her with such a strange, intent expression that she felt as though she couldn't' breathe.

The connection between Adam's expression and her own rapidly beating heart was beyond Marina. Perhaps it was a sort of possession.

Yes, that would explain it. It wasn't really Marina's hand reaching out towards him, letting her fingertips skim the bristled surface of his cheek, and the sharp line of his jaw.

Adam's breath caught in his throat. Marina couldn't remember the last time she'd breathed at all.

He leaned forward, slowly and carefully, and Marina tilted her face towards him.

Their lips fitted together perfectly. It was barely a brush of skin on soft skin, but it sent Marina's heart hammering wildly. Adam pulled back; eyes wide.

"I..." he began.

Then the door opened, and Mrs Brown stepped into the room.

"The doctor has gone, your Graces. He said to tell you that..." she began, cheerfully unaware of what she'd just done.

Adam leapt to his feet; face bright red. Marina hardly dared imagine what she looked like.

"Do excuse me." He said, voice short and sharp. Without waiting for a reply, Adam turned on his heel and strode out of the door, closing it firmly behind him.

Mrs Brown blinked. "Well. That was odd, wasn't it, your Grace?"

Chapter Twenty-Eight

Three Days Later

The little parlour, decorated in shades of pink, turned out to be the perfect place for Marina to spend her days. It was comfortable, warm, quiet, and pretty.

Adam also avoided the place like the plague.

Marina couldn't think of anything but their kiss. She had touched him. He had kissed her. Then Mrs Brown had appeared, and Adam had run for the hills. He hadn't joined her for dinner that night, and Marina had ultimately learned through poor Julian that Adam had packed up and gone to stay in the dower house.

It was simpler for his work, he said.

She didn't believe a single word of it. Whatever the motivation behind that kiss, it was clear that Adam regretted it. The two hadn't exchanged a single word beyond the obvious pleasantries when their paths crossed in the hallway.

Mrs Brown clearly knew that something was up but didn't seem to want to openly ask. That was fair. Marina was relieved she hadn't asked.

With something of a sixth sense, Geraldine had known to stop suggesting the pretty dresses for Marina to wear, or the newest hairstyles. When the flower had disappeared from its vase on Marina's nightstand, Geraldine didn't bother asking why.

Marina didn't know whether to be grateful or to resent their pity.

She sat in the little pink room, trying to concentrate on a book, while Geraldine worked on some sewing.

Infuriatingly, it didn't seem to matter how often Marina read the same page. The words squiggled together into ink-black lines of gibberish, and she hadn't turned a page in at least twenty minutes.

She glanced at the clock. It was hours yet until dinner, and it would be hours after that until she could reasonably retire to her room. The day stretched ahead of her, dull, boring, and full of disappointment.

A gentle rap came on the door. Marina allowed herself a moment to imagine that it might be Adam, before she remembered that he hadn't set foot in the house since they'd kissed, and now lived at the dower house, and would live there presumably until they returned to London.

No doubt Blackburn Manor had a dower house, too. Or perhaps he would just take up apartments in London.

"Come in." Marina called.

Julian stepped inside, carrying a letter on a silver tray.

"For you, your Grace." He said, stooping to let her pick up the letter.

Marina immediately recognized the blotchy, childish handwriting. A letter from Josephine, at last.

She tore open the seal and began to read.

My Dearest Marina

I hope you're well. I also hope that you're sitting down, because I'll tell you now that this letter doesn't contain any good news at all.

Are you sitting safely? Good. I'll begin.

Everything has gone wrong since you left London. We were all heartbroken to see you go, of course, and Papa was planning a trip to go up and visit you. I think he intended to invite himself to stay.

Then Lord Ellersby returned.

I'm sure you remember him. That nasty, cadaverous-looking man who always looks a bit like a curtain pole to me. Well, he found out that you were to marry the Duke, and he was exceptionally angry. The night after your wedding, he arrived at our home and barged his way inside. He demanded that he be given 'his reward' – yes, that is what he called you, Marina – and was quite livid to find out that you were already married.

He said that he would make Papa sorry and left.

Well, we thought it was just a threat. Papa seemed shaken, but not worried.

The bailiffs arrived at our house the next day.

Lord Ellersby had produced evidence of a debt that Papa owed him and claimed that your marriage to him ought to have written it off. Papa tried to argue, but there was no arguing with those bailiffs. He insisted that Lord Ellersby was a crook and a liar, but they wouldn't let us even look at those wretched documents.

The bailiffs marched Papa away.

The very next day, the judge sentenced him.

It was a very quick trial, and I would bet every penny of my dwindling inheritance that Lord Ellersby had bribed the judge.

The long and short of it is that Papa is in Marshalsea. We can't get in to see him, and nobody seems to want to listen to us. I don't know where to go or what to do, because Mama is now terribly ill.

She stood outside the gaol for hours in the rain and freezing cold, then stood in a damp little room inside the gaol for hours more before they would let her see Papa. After all that, she barely had ten minutes with him, enough to see that he was thoroughly miserable and living in squalid conditions.

Mama fell into a fever only a few hours after she returned. We pray that she didn't pick up something terrible form the prison. She is unconscious and delirious most of the time, and we can't afford a doctor. Whenever she is conscious, she asks for Papa at once. I've taken to lying to her and telling her that he's out for a walk instead of being stuck in prison, because she gets so distressed to hear that he's in prison.

I don't know what to do, Marina. I'm terrified for Papa, for Mama, and for myself. I beg you to come home. If you bring the Duke, he might be able to help us.

I'm using the last of my money to frank this and send it off with all haste. Please, please come back to London as soon as you get this.

All my love, your harried and panicking sister,
Josephine

Marina crumpled the letter in shaking hands, sucking in a sharp, ragged breath.

Geraldine looked up.

"Your Grace?" Her gaze dropped to the letter. "Is it bad news?"

Marina squeezed her eyes closed, nodding. She placed the letter on the coffee table, not wanting to touch it more than she had to. It was silly, but it felt as if the letter itself was somehow tainted.

Poor Josephine. She's all alone.

"It's very bad news. Ring the bell, please, Geraldine."

Only a few moments later, Mrs Brown appeared in the doorway. Her smile dropped off her face when she saw Marina's ashen expression.

"Your Grace, is something the matter?"

"My mother is extremely ill, and my father has been taken to Marshalsea." Marina said tightly. "It seems as if the charges against him are trumped-up, and he requires help. I must leave for London at once. Within the hour. Sooner, if possible. Please, will you have the carriage readied? Geraldine, pack a few of my things. Just the necessities."

Geraldine nodded, swallowing hard, and darted out of the room.

Mrs Brown remained, nibbling her lip and eyeing Marina nervously.

"This has shocked you, your Grace. Please, rest for a while."

Marina shook her head. "There's no time to waste."

Mrs Brown nodded. "Of course. I shall fetch his Grace immediately."

"No, wait. Don't bother his Grace."

She paused, frowning. "But his Grace may be in a position to..."

"No." Marina repeated, firmly. Adam had pushed her away and made it clear that he wanted nothing to do with her. Why should she go to him for help. "No, thank you, Mrs Brown. I shall handle this myself. Now, please, go and see about that carriage."

Mrs Brown dropped a curtsey, her expression neutral. "At once, your Grace. At once."

Chapter Twenty-Nine

The dower house hadn't been used in decades, and it clearly showed. The last person to live there had been... well, Adam couldn't remember. His own mother had died long before she could become a Dowager, and Evelyn had always just lived in the house.

The servants had done an excellent job of clearing up the place, of course. There was no musty smell hanging in the air. The floors were swept, the surfaces dusted, the fireplace clean and ready for a good blaze, and the linens were fresh and not damp in the slightest.

But there was something about a long-abandoned place that couldn't just be cleaned away like dust. Something damp and sad hung in the air. The dower house was always cold, even in the brightest sunshine, and never seemed to welcome a person home the way other houses did.

It's your imagination, Adam told himself firmly. You can imagine what Father would think of letting your imagination run wild.

That was an excellent point. The old Duke had never had any patience at all to imagined monsters under the bed or hiding in shadows. He was of the believe that one's fellow man was the real monster and was determined to inculcate that belief in his son.

For the most part, he had succeeded.

There was no proper study in the dower house, only a writing desk in the corner of the only parlour. It wasn't a comfortable spot. It was cramped and inconvenient, but it was that or sit on the sofa.

Adam leaned over one of the ledgers – the large book barely fitted onto the writing desk, which was clearly designed for a lady and her moderate writing needs in mind – and blinked hard, rubbing his eyes with the back of his hand.

The sun was going on, creating that strange sort of half-twilight that made it so difficult to see. He'd lit candles, of course, but nothing seemed to do the trick. The dower house was a place that was always cold, always dark.

I'll be glad to get out, Adam thought grimly.

Despite his childhood imagination having been thoroughly suppressed, a sharp knock at the door made him jump out of his skin. Various scenarios flashed through his mind, including but not limited to escaped, murderous lunatics, bandits, and various monsters that his imagination conjured up.

Adam stood warily behind the door, wishing that his valet wasn't over at the main house.

"Who is it?" he called.

"It's me, your Grace. It's Mrs Brown."

He grinned in relief, shaking his head at himself. Adam unlocked the door and opened it. Mrs Brown stepped in immediately, not waiting to be asked.

It was apparent that something was wrong. Something serious.

Adam's smile faded.

"Mrs Brown? What is it?"

She was out of breath, and a little dishevelled from running. She clutched a crumpled letter in her hand.

"I... I know it might not be my place, your Grace." Mrs Brown gasped, "But I thought you'd better look at this. This letter arrived for her Grace the Duchess about an hour ago. I've only just had the opportunity to bring it to you."

Adam blinked, not sure how to take this. On the one hand, he ought to tell her off for such a breach of privacy. On the other hand, Mrs Brown would never do something like this without good reason.

"Well, let me read it, then."

She pushed the letter into his hand and stood back, waiting.

The colour drained from Adam's face as he read. His father-in-law was in Marshalsea on charges that were undoubtedly trumped-up. He'd cleared the man's debts himself.

However, the legal system could be distinctly unfriendly in cases like this. The Cornish had no money to grease palms, no influence, no power. Their name had been sinking steadily over the years, and now poor Samuel Cornish would be no better than a common debtor. With the powerful Lord Ellersby pursuing him, he'd have no chance at getting out of prison, especially without his wife to help him.

Letitia Cornish's illness sounded severe. Doctors were expensive, but if she didn't get medical help soon… he drew in a deep breath. The letter was horribly crumpled, as if someone had twisted it up into a ball between their hands.

He could only imagine how Marina had felt upon reading this letter.

"Do you know the contents of this letter?" he asked Mrs Brown.

She shook her head. "I have not read it myself, your Grace. I only know what her Grace told me. She was exceedingly panicked. She ordered the carriage and desired her maid to pack up and be ready to leave within the hour."

Adam frowned. "This is the first I'm hearing of it. Surely she must have sent word to me, if we're to leave together."

Mrs Brown averted her eyes, and Adam realized the truth.

"She didn't intend to leave with you." Mrs Brown replied calmly. "She didn't intend to tell you."

Adam swallowed hard, unconsciously crumpling the poor letter in his hand. Again.

Should he be surprised? He'd worked diligently to push Marina away, to make it clear that their marriage was one of convenience, and that they would lead separate lives. He shouldn't be surprised to find that she had no intention of going to him for help at a time like this.

"Your Grace?" Mrs Brown asked, her eyes wide. "Are you going to help her?"

Adam raked a hand through his hair. The gesture would make it stick up comically, but he didn't care.

"I must speak to her at once. Where is she?"

Mrs Brown swallowed. "She left not fifteen minutes ago, your Grace."

A muscle jumped in Adam's jaw.

"Then have my horse saddled up at once." He said levelly. "There's no time to waste."

***

It was fully dark now. Adam's stomach, used to eating dinner at this time, grumbled in complaint.

The horse was one of his favourites, a glossy black mare by the name of Blackberry. Blackberry was a fine, strong horse, and one of the fastest beasts in the stable. That was the main reason that Adam had chosen her.

He had a good chance of catching the carriage, even with their head start, even with the growing dark.

The real danger, of course, was that they would reach the Brixham Fork before he could catch up. That was where the road diverged, and both ways would lead in the direction that Marina wanted to go. The left fork was substantially quicker, but the right one was safer, and smoother for the carriage. Which one would she take?

Blackberry galloped through the night, surefooted on the uneven road. Adam hung on, leaning forward and squinting forward through the dark. He was vaguely aware that going alone was a bad idea. If he took a tumble, he could lie in a ditch for hours before anyone ever realized that he was in danger.

The Brixham Fork appeared, and Adam skidded to a halt.

Damn, he thought, a very ungentlemanly work. Now what?

He peered down both forks in hopes of spotting the bobbing pinprick of a carriage lantern.

There was nothing.

Adam drew in a deep breath, and spurred Blackberry down the left fork. The road immediately narrowed, becoming barely wide enough for a carriage to pass by, and the ground underneath turned rutted and uneven.

Come on, Marina, Adam thought desperately. Please don't let me lose you.

Chapter Thirty

The carriage rolled over an exceptionally deep pothole, sending both Marina and Geraldine lurching forward.

"Ouch." Marina muttered, rubbing the back of her neck. "I'm going to be too sore to walk when we get there. I'm sorry, Geraldine, I shouldn't have made you come."

Geraldine looked vaguely affronted at this. "I am your lady's maid, your Grace. Where you go, I go."

"Well, I can't say I'm sorry to have your company. It's going to be a long drive home. Maybe you and I can figure out a way to get Papa out of Marshalsea."

That was supposed to be a light-hearted remark, but Geraldine didn't smile. Marina didn't feel like smiling, either.

She had no idea how to get Samuel free. She had a little money, but not much. Would that be enough to pay for a doctor for Letitia? Marina wished that she'd brought some of the jewels Adam had brought her. She could have sold them, at least.

A pang went through her chest at the thought of Adam. Would he find out where she'd gone? Marina had written him a note, but then crumpled it up and thrown it away. He wouldn't care, and he would be too busy here to come down to London anyway.

Where do we go from here? Marina thought dully. I'll be in London, and he'll be in Brixham. Will he care? Will he miss me? I doubt it. Maybe he'll decide on an annulment.

Geraldine suddenly sat bolt upright, reaching out to grab Marina's arm.

"Do you hear that?" she whispered.

"Hear what?"

"Hoofbeats. It must be bandits!"

"It won't be bandits." Marina insisted, although a cold surge of fear went through her.

Geraldine's eyes were wide and terrified. "I told you we should have taken the right fork, your Grace."

Then the carriage lurched to a halt, and the two women clutched at each other, terrified.

Marina swallowed hard. The carriage curtains were pulled

down, and with the lantern in the corner, their world seemed to shrink to the tiny space. She strained her ears for gunshots, for raised voices, for anything.

Geraldine was right, though – there were hoofbeats.

Marina slid her hand underneath the seat, where a small but serviceable pistol resided. It had been a present from Samuel years ago, and Marina was sure that she could fire it if need be.

She took out the pistol and levelled it at the window opposite.

Geraldine gulped audibly.

"Are you sure you know what you're doing, your Grace?" she whispered.

Marina nodded, despite feeling nothing of the sort.

"We're not getting robbed and murdered today, Geraldine." She murmured.

Then the door behind them opened suddenly, and the two women screamed.

Marina swung the pistol around, just in time to see Adam dive to the side.

"Good Lord, Marina!" he cried. "Don't shoot. It's me. It's me!"

"Oh. It is you." Marina managed, her face turning an intriguing shade of red. "I thought you were bandits."

Adam peered around the corner of the carriage.

"No. It's me."

Marina set down the pistol with a shaking hand, not sure whether she wanted to laugh or cry.

"So I see. Why are you here, Adam?"

"I might ask you the same."

Marina bit her lip, looking away. "It's none of your concern."

He sighed. "Step outside, Marina. I want to talk to you."

Marina considered telling him she would do nothing of the sort, and then instructing the coachman to drive on. She decided against it, mostly because she wasn't sure the coachman would obey. She climbed down from the carriage and closed the door behind her, leaving the whimpering Geraldine to calm down in peace.

Adam wordlessly held up the letter Josephine had sent.

Marina swallowed again. "That was private."

"Your father is in Marshalsea, and your mother is seriously ill. Why did you not tell me, Marina?"

She folded her arms. "Would you have stopped me from coming?"

"Stopped you? Good heavens, of course not! I would have helped you."

"Why should I believe that?" Marina snapped. "It's clear that you want nothing to do with me. You avoid me at every turn. One moment you seem to genuinely enjoy my company, and the next you can't even look at me. I'm tired of it, Adam. I can't live like that. I cannot trust you."

She broke up, eyeing him nervously. Would Adam be angry at her outburst?

His expression was unreadable. Folding the letter carefully, Adam placed it in his breast pocket, and reached out to take Marina's hands in his.

"I have not been trustworthy." He admitted. "You're right. I haven't been consistent in the way I have treated you. I was hurt, just now, when I learned that you hadn't come to me for help, but I can't blame you for that. The truth is..." he paused, closing his eyes. "The truth is, Marina, I was brought up to believe that affection is weakness. That a true man – a nobleman, no less – never apologises, never shows any sort of weakness, and never needs anyone in any way. I watched my parents' love wane and fade away completely, because of my father's stubbornness. Because of the qualities his father instilled in him. It's been going on for generations, like a sickness."

Marina had a strong urge to fling her arms around him. She settled for staring up at him, eyes wide.

"You aren't a cruel man. You aren't weak, either."

"I am weak in some ways. You make me weak." Adam smiled softly, taking a step closer. "I... I am in love with you, Marina."

She sucked in a breath, sure that she must have misheard.

"I beg your pardon?"

"I love you, Marina." Adam repeated, his voice stronger this time. "I suppose it scared me. My mother loved my father, you know, and it hurt her more than she ever let on. I suppose I was afraid that I would end up like that, but all that happened was that I turned into my father."

"You aren't like him." Marina said vehemently. "Everyone else says that too, so it isn't just me who thinks it. You're a good man, Adam."

He smiled weakly. "I try. But that's the truth, Marina. If you don't feel the same about me, I will never, ever use our marriage as leverage against you. You can go your own way and live your own life, and I will never hurt you in any way. But please, if there is hope, please tell me now."

Marina wanted to laugh.

"Hope?" she giggled. "Hope?"

Anxiety was just starting to show itself on his face when Marina stood up on her tiptoes, cupped Adam's face in her palms, and kissed him full on the mouth.

"I love you too, you wretched man." She breathed, laughter still bubbling up inside her. "We're a pair of fools, aren't we?"

Adam wrapped his arms around her waist, grinning.

"We certainly are. Now, much as I'd love to stand here and kiss you all night, I believe we have your father to save from Marshalsea, and a doctor to procure for you mother."

Marina smiled. "Yes, I believe we do. Shall we go?"

Epilogue

The Following Day

Lord Ellersby was having a very good day indeed. First, he'd triumphed over that back-stabbing Lord Chelwood, and now Chelwood's delectable daughter had chosen to take matters into her own hands.

He'd received her note only that morning. It was carefully written, but Lord Ellersby had always been good at reading between the lines.

It was ridiculous, marrying a girl like that off to the Duke of Brixham. When it came to breeding, it was like pairing a common mare with a fine, purebred stallion.

Of course, the Chelwood girl was very beautiful, and pleasantly young, too, whereas the Duke was said to be a cold fish. It wasn't a surprise to hear that the young Marina was back in London, without her husband.

She was keen to do what was necessary to get her father released from Marshalsea, and Lord Ellersby was in a mood to be persuaded. It was a pity he couldn't actually marry the girl, but there were other fish in the sea.

He skipped up the steps to the Chelwood house two at a time, humming tunelessly under his breath.

The butler, dislike seething under his carefully constructed impassive expression, opened the door without a word. Lord Ellersby threw his coat and hat at the man, not bothering to look at him.

The younger Chelwood girl, whose name he could never remember, was waiting in the hallway, arms folded. She had a face like thunder. She was pretty enough, and Lord Ellersby had briefly considered asking for her hand instead.

He'd decided against it. He liked Marina best, and the younger girl had the air of someone who might put arsenic in his food.

"Where is your sister? We have business." He said brusquely.

"The parlour." The girl shot back. "You ought to be ashamed

of yourself."

Lord Ellersby flashed her a smile. He wondered if he should tell her that her obvious dislike was like meat and drink to him.

"How is your darling mama, then? Dead yet?"

The girl gave a tight-lipped smile.

"She's recovering quickly. Marina brought in a very good doctor for her. She's awake now."

He eyed her face for a moment, searching for signs that she was putting on a brave face, hopefully to take away the enjoyment of his knowing that Letitia Cornish was on her deathbed.

There was no hint of a lie in the young girl's face. Obviously, her Mama really was recovering.

Ah. Disappointing. Still, no matter. Lord Ellersby shrugged and pushed his way past the girl towards the parlour. The girl didn't follow him.

He shouldered open the parlour door, and stood in the doorway, grinning.

Marina Cornish — although it was Marina Blackburn now, wasn't it? — sat on an armchair opposite the door. She was wearing a travel-crumpled grey dress and was clearly exhausted, but still looked as pretty as ever. He grinned at her.

"Ah, my dear Marina."

"That's your Grace to you."

He chuckled. "Such spirit! Although not really the correct attitude here."

Marina raised an eyebrow. "And what's the correct attitude, then?"

He shrugged. "Penitence, perhaps? You and I had an arrangement, my dear. Such contracts ought not to be entered into lightly. You broke the contract, and now must pay the price."

"Interesting that you mention price, Lord Ellersby. You had my father thrown into Marshalsea because of unpaid debts, but his debts were paid off at the event of my marriage."

"Alas, no." Lord Ellersby said, injecting a suitable amount of regret into his voice. It wouldn't do to be too gleeful. "Not all debts, I'm afraid. Don't blame yourself, my dear. You weren't to know. Ladies don't have the head for numbers. Neither, it seems, does your poor Papa. It certainly wounded me to have him punished so harshly, but debt is a serious thing. I'm sure that you and I can come to an arrangement."

She raised her eyebrow again. The motion was starting to annoy him, not to mention the fact that she hadn't invited him to sit. If they were to further their acquaintance – and Lord Ellersby had no doubt that they would, if she wanted her father to ever set foot outside of Marshalsea again – she had better improve her manners. She had better smile more, too, and wipe that disdainful expression off her face.

In fact, that expression was beginning to annoy him. He took a step forward, glad that the younger Chelwood girl hadn't seen fit to follow him. It was better that it was just him and Marina.

"You aren't as grateful as I expected."

She laughed. Actually laughed. The peal of laughter almost made Lord Ellersby flinch.

"Grateful? For what? For putting my father in gaol for these imagined debts? You could get into a great deal of trouble, Lord Ellersby."

He wasn't smiling now. His good mood had gone, like a balloon pricked with a needle, and it was all Marina Cornish's fault. He took another step forward.

"Listen here, you empty-headed girl. I'm prepared to use my influence to get your dear papa out of Marshalsea, but in return, you're going to have to be much more obliging to me than this."

He'd expected – even looked forward to – the expression of dawning horror on Marina's face, assuming she hadn't already worked out how this was going to go.

He was disappointed. Marina inspected her nails, not even flinching.

"I think not." she said sweetly.

"My dear girl..."

"I must remind you again, Lord Ellersby, that you will address me as your Grace."

His patience was running out. Lord Ellersby stepped forward, quite ready to teach the chit a lesson.

The door slammed behind him, making him jump.

He spun around and noticed for the first time a second occupant of the room. It was a man, sitting on a seat directly behind the door, so that Lord Ellersby wouldn't see him right away. He was tall, handsome, well-built, and had a face like stone.

"Who is this? You promised a private audience." Lord Ellersby snapped.

The man didn't respond. He kept his gaze firmly on Lord Ellersby, not even blinking. It was disconcerting.

"The thing about the debt my father supposedly owes you." Marina said, her voice speculative, "Is that he doesn't owe anyone money. Not anymore. His debts were paid off. This gentleman here is the one who paid them off, you see. He and his lawyers are very interested to hear about this debt. Since you had my father indicted on the strength of the evidence of this debt, I'm sure you'll have no problem at all providing it. And no doubt it will stand up to close scrutiny."

Lord Ellersby finally understood who the man in the room was. He paled.

The man smiled. It was an unpleasant, wolfish sort of smile.

"My name is Lord Adam Blackburn, Duke of Brixham. I believe you've heard of me."

Lord Ellersby swallowed hard. He was in trouble. Serious trouble. That wretched judge would sing like a bird as soon as the Duke showed his face. It would all come out – the bribes, the falsification of documents... no, this wasn't good at all.

He turned back to Marina, and forced what he hoped was a pleasant, friendly smile.

"I'm sure this isn't necessary. Listen, my dear girl..."

She leaned forward, flashing the same wolfish smile as her husband.

"For the last time, Lord Ellersby. You had really better call me your Grace."

Extended Epilogue

One Year Later, Blackburn Manor

It never ceased to amaze Adam how quickly life could change. In the space of a single year, his life had been turned on its head. All for the better, of course.

He'd neatly secured his in-laws admiration and respect by ordering a doctor for Letitia and neatly springing Samuel from gaol.

And then, just as neatly, replacing the innocent Samuel with the much less innocent Lord Ellersby. Between the crimes of bribery, blackmail, falsification of documents, and a whole host of other less savoury crimes, Lord Ellersby would be spending the rest of his life in gaol.

Adam was very pleased about that.

He was startled out of his reverie by Josephine, bouncing along the hallway.

"Any news?" she asked breathlessly. "Mama won't tell me anything."

Adam shook his head. "Doctor Severn and the midwife assures me that the labour is going along very well. Your sister will be fine, Josephine."

Josephine didn't look convinced. She took a seat on the long bench beside Adam, the two of them sitting in the hallway outside the master bedroom.

The door was closed, and nobody but the midwife, the doctor, and Letitia had been allowed in.

"I wish they'd let me in with her." Adam said, after a pause. "I know that a man like me will probably get in the way, but I could hold her hand. I could support her."

Josephine pulled a face. "I wouldn't want to go in. All that blood and screaming."

Adam swallowed hard.

He'd spent most of Marina's pregnancy thinking about the things that could go wrong. Marina herself didn't seem to be nervous. And now the big day was here.

I'm going to be a father, Adam thought, the idea accompanied by a stifling rush of panic.

He wasn't ready. He couldn't be a father. What if he made mistakes, like his father had with him, and his father with him?

"There's so much that can go wrong." Adam whispered, clenched his hands into fists.

Josephine slipped her arm through his.

"Don't worry." She murmured. "They'll be fine."

On cue, a thin, reedy cry started up from inside the room. Adam's heart was in his mouth.

They waited for a breathless ten minutes before the door opened, and Doctor Severn appeared, smiling broadly.

"All is well, your Grace. You have a healthy son, and her Grace is also in good health. Would you like to come in?"

Adam's breath stuttered.

"I... yes. Yes, I would. Please."

He followed the doctor inside, barely noticing the chaos of the room.

Marina was lying in bed, exhausted. Blankets and pillows were piled up around her, and her hair stuck to her forehead with sweat. A tiny bundle was wrapped up in her arms.

Letitia, folding up some blood-soaked towels, caught Adam's eye, and smiled tearfully at him.

"He's beautiful." She sniffled. "Take a look."

Adam shuffled to Marina's bedside, feeling strangely out of place.

She smiled up at him, eyes dark-ringed and exhausted.

"Did the doctor tell you? A little boy."

"How are you, my love?" Adam whispered, leaning down to kiss her forehead.

Marina pulled a face. "Sore, to say the least. I feel as though I haven't slept for a week. Although the first time I saw him, I couldn't think of anything else beside him. Take a look, Adam. He's got your eyes."

Adam stared down at the tiny bundle in his wife's arms.

The baby was a mottled red colour, with wisps of damp, black hair sticking up from his soft scalp. His minute hands were curled into fists at his chest, and his eyes were shut.

"He's frowning." Adam said.

Marina snorted. "He's taking after you already."

She cackled at her own joke, and the baby opened dim, unfocused eyes at the noise, glancing around the room as if to ascertain the source of the disturbance.

Hesitantly, Adam extended a finger towards the baby. Its tiny hand clamped around his finger, tightening with impressive strength.

"That's... that's a firm grip." Adam said, surprised.

Marina smiled. "Yes, I've heard that about babies. Do you want to hold him?"

"Yes. I want to hold him."

The words were out before Adam could think about it. He couldn't put a name to it, the warm, aching feeling in his chest that bloomed whenever he looked at his brand-new son. He couldn't take his eyes away from the baby. It was similar to what he felt for Marina, but also completely different, at the same time.

Something powerful. Something primal.

She gently placed the baby into his arms, and Adam held him close to his chest.

The baby was heavier than he'd expected, warm. Its eyes were still open, fingers curling vaguely in the air.

"I thought he'd be crying and screaming." Adam said. "Father said that babies did nothing but scream."

"Well, I'm sure we'll have our fair share of screaming, but babies certainly do more than that." Marina huffed, gingerly turning to lie on her side. She smiled up at Adam, her eyes soft. "Isn't he beautiful?"

"The most beautiful baby I've ever seen in my life." Adam said fervently. "The most beautiful baby that ever was."

"I concur." Marina grinned. "So, let's think of names. Had we decided between Jasper and Thomas for a boy?"

Adam touched the whisper-soft hair on the top of the baby's head.

"I don't mind what you call him. You can choose."

Marina bit her lip. "I thought you might have wanted to name him after your father."

Adam caught her eye. "I think perhaps our baby ought to be

his own person."

Marina smiled. "I agree. I love you, Adam."

He bent down to kiss her, careful not to jostle the new baby.

"I love you too, Marina. I never imagined I would have this – a wife I loved, a baby. A family."

She let her fingers dance along his jawline.

"You'll never be alone again." she murmured. "You've found your place. We both have."

The End

Made in United States
North Haven, CT
30 June 2025